PENGUIN
THE DIARY OF AN U.

Madhav Mathur is a banker by d   ... —ilm-maker by
night. He divides his time between Delhi, his hometown, and
Singapore, where he lives and works. He means well but doesn't
sound like it.

THE DIARY OF AN UNREASONABLE MAN

Madhav Mathur

PENGUIN BOOKS

PENGUIN BOOKS
Published by the Penguin Group
Penguin Books India Pvt. Ltd, 11 Community Centre, Panchsheel Park,
New Delhi 110 017, India
Penguin Group (USA) Inc., 375 Hudson Street, New York, New York 10014, USA
Penguin Group (Canada), 90 Eglinton Avenue East, Suite 700, Toronto,
Ontario, M4P 2Y3, Canada (a division of Pearson Penguin Canada Inc.)
Penguin Books Ltd, 80 Strand, London WC2R 0RL, England
Penguin Ireland, 25 St Stephen's Green, Dublin 2, Ireland
(a division of Penguin Books Ltd)
Penguin Group (Australia), 250 Camberwell Road, Camberwell,
Victoria 3124, Australia (a division of Pearson Australia Group Pty Ltd)
Penguin Group (NZ), 67 Apollo Drive, Rosedale, North Shore 0632, New Zealand
(a division of Pearson New Zealand Ltd)
Penguin Group (South Africa) (Pty) Ltd, 24 Sturdee Avenue, Rosebank,
Johannesburg 2196, South Africa

Penguin Books Ltd, Registered Offices: 80 Strand, London WC2R 0RL, England

First published by Penguin Books India 2009

Copyright © Madhav Mathur 2009

All rights reserved

10 9 8 7 6 5 4 3 2 1

ISBN 9780143068136

This is a work of fiction. Names, characters, places and incidents are either the product
of the author's imagination or are used fictitiously and any resemblance to any actual
person, living or dead, events or locales is entirely coincidental.

Typeset in Goudy Old Style by SÜRYA, New Delhi
Printed at Thomson Press India Ltd, New Delhi

For my Baba and Nana.
Thank you for sharing your love of the written word with me.
I miss you both.

'The reasonable man adapts himself to the world; the unreasonable one persists in trying to adapt the world to himself. Therefore all progress depends on the unreasonable man.'

—George Bernard Shaw, *Man and Superman*

CONTENTS

x   Contents

ACKNOWLEDGEMENTS

I would like to thank Avanija, my supportive and gutsy editor, and Pushkar, my cover designer and good friend, who've given *The Diary of an Unreasonable Man* its final form. I would also like to thank Rachna, my resourceful and creative publicist. Thanks are also due to my sister Shivani for her patience and honesty, my parents and Dadima for their guidance, and, of course, my friends for tolerating me. A very special thank you to Anurag Kashyap for all his support and for his generous praise for the book.

1. THE BEGINNING OF THE END

This could have been a good ride. This could even have been perfect. But the knife-like elbows of my neighbour, digging into my sides, coupled with his inordinate love for flatulent indiscretions made it otherwise. Almost half the compartment turned to glare at him. He smiled sheepishly and twiddled his thumbs. They were opposable, I checked.

I watched the people who shared the moving tin box with me. My fellow sardines, mildly salted for the vicious piranhas that they worked for. Expressways were jammed with more worker ants crawling over each other to begin their day's labour. Familiar sights that had now become associated with getting to work adorned the ever-changing canvas that was our compartment window. The same trio of children taking a dump on the side of the tracks, the same girl fighting in various degrees of agitation to board our iron ark, the same billboard in disrepair, I knew them all. I had made them an important part of my day today, even though there weren't any piranhas waiting for me. Not any more.

Looking around at the people in the compartment with me I was struck by how dejected and morose some of them looked. Bored faces, mirrors of minds dulled by repetition, sat before me, staring. Some were barely awake, looking out of the window expectantly. A few were lost in their dreams, holding on desperately to those five extra minutes of sweet vital slumber. Others read the morning paper, the 'V' of their eyebrows pointed in an air of distinguished concentration as they strained their eyes to read the articles before them, looking for anecdotes that would serve as fodder for their lunchtime discussions and bitching sessions.

Every person seemed to have his own planet to save and everyone's world was close to crumbling. A sea of a million Atlases in office attire, lined the walls. Blue shirt, white shirt, pink shirt, white shirt . . . Bag, bag, bag. It was an undulating monotony of pigments differing from one another only slightly. They swayed gently, like a cheesy Republic Day demonstration with hundreds of young people waving cuttings of fabric, as the characteristic tremble of the carriage rocked us all to the same song.

There were schoolchildren chattering endlessly to my left. The more ill-behaved ones chose to play a game of hide-and-seek in the middle of the compartment, screaming, teasing each other, using other passengers as pillars to hide behind. The rather large lady in front of me tried shaking them off. The little gentleman engulfed in the drapes of her sari was undeterred. He found her to be his best and most effective means for concealment. We all watched as the little marauders kept themselves busy. Their disgruntled parents seemed to have given up on order. They sat scratching themselves, waiting for the next stop, much like proud lions wallowing in their magnificence on one of those National Geographic shows. Watching their regal offspring make short work of the surroundings. This was their kingdom, was it not?

A few seats down, young women on their way to college sported the latest in trendy campus wear. I've never understood fashion, never quite been on the cutting edge of glamour myself. I don't understand the need to blend in yet stand out and all that carefully crafted drivel. These days a nose ring, hair colour or tattoo expresses who we are. It's pointless to argue because Rohit Bal said so.

I sat there waiting for the next stop, rocking away. There was a countdown in my head, Beethoven's 9th playing slowly. I thought of Picasso's beautiful blue phase, his meditative cerulean introspection. I thought of 'The Old Guitarist' despondently seated with his instrument. To me he was a lost old man, clinging on to whatever little he could. That used to be me, staring down at the floor, looking for answers and acceptance. Not from anyone else, just from myself. That was me, a victim, searching for something to define me and pull me out of my depression, something that would give me the courage to change my life, to put down the laptop bag and think.

I had a couple of choices back then.

I could easily have become the dejected Devdas, Saratchandra's immortal character, the embodiment of unrequited love, the figurehead of a life wasted, drowning my woes in alcohol. A cigarette and booze-totting spokesman for surrender introducing my only two friends Philip, Philip Morris, and Glen, Glenfiddich to one and all.

Abandoned by hope and joy, I would be destroyed by disease and dissipation. I would have spent the better part of my days building cigarette butt Stonehenges in the middle of my drawing room wasteland, monuments to commemorate and celebrate my nothingness.

Or, I could have chosen to become like the loud, energetic, hormonally driven 'worldly' white boy, a desi Stiffler straight out of a Mumbai version of the American Pie trilogy. Chasing skirts and living in the moment. Accepting the superficiality of my existence and doing all that I could to juice it and extract a shallow momentary sense of happiness.

But that too was not for me. I needed more.

I couldn't be defined by past failings or by the much-touted 'moment'. People of note often talk about the 'moment' and all the potential it has. To me, if you live in the moment, you're likely to waver in terms of purpose and meaning. Call me foolish, but I needed something larger in my life, something to live and die for. I needed a plan. Sure you do what you have to in the moment, but it should all add up to something larger. I was tired of merely feeling strongly about the things around me. I wanted to act for my cause. I could no longer walk in circles, pontificate, pay rent, buy cheese and resume my romp in the endless arc.

I wondered how many faces in front of me stopped to think about what they were doing and why. More importantly, what or who was making them do that.

Fortunately for me the choice had already been made. It became clearer to me as the days went by. Justified and clarified by life's 'fuck you' quality. With billboard-like visibility and hypnotic recall value.

I had decided about a year ago that my life had to mean more. That the drive and idealism of my schooldays would not die.

I quit my job.

Beethoven's 9th became louder and I couldn't contain my excitement as the train slowed down by the platform. Hawkers fried tikkis outside. Kids ran along the platform with the train. People pushed and shoved to position themselves for the optimum angle of approach to dive into the carriage. Fruit-juice sellers were peddling their jaundice, as magazine men palmed off the intricate details of film stars' chinaware. The station was untamed and alive.

'Dadar Central,' the electronic woman said over the intercom.

I got up and started for the exit, crowds of people were entangled in an uncontrollable mass now, pressed into each other near the doors. I squeezed out and started walking. It was right on time. Of course, I had accounted for the four-minute delay that crept into the system every morning.

The bomb went off with a thunderous clap.

The compartment shook violently as the thick liquid made its way in every direction, plastering everything and everyone. Fountains of paint flew angrily and the screams that surrounded me grew louder as I walked away calmly. Some of the glass panes gave way and fell out behind me.

'Bomb!'

'Fuck! It's a bomb!'

'Oh god, it's a bomb!'

'Get out! Get out!'

'Run!'

'Get the hell out now!'

A flurry of shouted commands bounced around liberally garnished with expletives. Ironically, the sounds of the expletives mingled with the screams of people calling out to god. To each his own, I guess.

The smile became hard to contain now. Ear to ear, they could've clicked me for a corny toothpaste commercial, had I not pulled out a cigarette and lit it in celebration. Leaflets flew all over the place, as though it were raining paper behind me.

A chaos ensued as men and women examined themselves for wounds. Taken by surprise, some cried as they couldn't believe what was happening. A couple of men ran out shrieking. Some held back others in protective gestures of heroism. No one was hurt. Shocked and anguished they crawled out of the compartment, covered in my favourite blue, mixing with the dirt and muck that encases and embellishes most of our train stations.

'Am I dead? Am I dead!'

'Calm down, sir, please . . .'

The paint had spread evenly all over. Wiping the emulsion of tears and paint from their faces crowds of startled men and women huddled together. Cries got louder as the police reached the scene. The window of the carriage was smeared with paint, accidental modern art. The shirts too were now all the same colour. A mother held her children tightly as they wept in her arms. A despondent-looking man stood staring at the ground, shaking in tears.

A stream of Persian blue flowed out from the compartment, forming mini tributaries that crept forward. A man followed it out, sticking to the ground, paranoia marking his face. The crowds that had lined the sides of the compartment had backed up. The only people reluctantly coming to their aid were the brave men in uniform at the station. A hysterical lady was flung out at their feet by the impatient mob.

'Are you hurt, ma'am? Can you breathe?' they frantically enquired.

Not many could hear them, the blast had blocked out their capacity to hear. It was like a forced sense of clarity, demanding attention towards only the sights around them.

'No one seems to be injured, sir; they are all in shock . . .'

'What about this glass?'

'It's from the train window . . .'

'Get me a fucking doctor!'

The havaldar followed orders and stepped away from the fray to ask for a medic, only to be interrupted by his boss.

'Is this blue chemical poisonous? Get on it! Find out if this stuff is poisonous . . .' enquired the horrified senior officer as he cupped his mouth and nose in sudden desperation.

The woman he was comforting began trembling even more now, her eyes were bloodshot and her mouth was wide open.

'Ambulances are on their way, ma'am, please don't worry . . .'

'Please stand back, secure the area, I want everyone searched and checked.'

'Fucking terrorists, what kind of new trick is this now?'

The men who had shrieked earlier, pushing women and children aside to clear their passage for escape, now donned quixotic enthusiasm and stepped forward.

'Terrorists! Goddam terrorists!'

'Why won't they leave us alone?'

They gave speeches and pointed fingers.

Everyone had so much to say. To be heard over the noise, in a concise, clear and memorable way, you need skill. You need a strong and consistent 'campaign'. Unfortunately too many people believe that you need to take lives in order to be taken seriously. That was not my intention. I choose not to slay, merely to remind and reform. To shake us and to crack through the seemingly impervious membrane that engulfs us in our disgustingly elaborate acquired zones of comfort. I was never going to hurt anyone.

Half the things I did would have been attributed to Osama and his mama hiding in the Bahamas. That's why I left them the leaflets.

They fluttered around until people gained their senses and picked them up. It was a beautiful sight. I paused for a moment to make sure they realized who it was from.

An old blue man lifted the paper and began reading.

I thought a simple title like 'Your Score' would be sufficiently dramatic.

This is how it read on what was meant to be the front:

Your Score
This near-death experience was brought to you by the Anarchists of Mumbai.

> *What if this was really the end?*
> *What if this explosion had ended your life?*
> *What if this had been your last journey?*
> *Start anew.*
> *Clean Yourself.*
> *Love and prayers,*
> *Your Anarchists*

The old man flipped the piece of paper over slowly.

> **We are all headed in the same direction.**
> **Quit the magazines. Forget your television.**
> **Re-evaluate!**
> **You are not a consumer, citizen.**
> **You are not a statistic.**
> **Think about what you do.**
> **Think about your reasons.**
> *Love and prayers,*
> *Your Anarchists*

They caught on. A policeman reading over the old man's shoulder yelled.

'It's the Anarchists again!'

He bent down to pick up another leaflet and read it again. He then looked back at the crowd of people soaked in paint. He shook his head furiously and started running towards the crowd, shouting out to his men.

'Seal off the exits; no one gets out of the station!'

It was time to leave.

Every month, there'd be a new Reader's Digest magazine delivered at my doorstep. The cover, without fail, would boast of intriguing, inspiring tales of shark attacks, grizzly bear assaults and light-aircraft-related near-death experiences. These experiences changed the lives of the people writing in. Would there be one titled 'I thought I was going to die in a train compartment' next month? We sure hoped so.

There had been some appreciation for our work in the recent past, by those who understood it in its entirety. The rest, we were still trying to reach out to. We made the news a lot, but of course, only as the Anarchists of Mumbai.

2. THE BEGINNING

My life had become a long, arduous practical joke.

An alarm went off. It was the usual annoying-by-design beep on repeat. After a while, it sounded like the latter half of Tool's epic 'Eulogy'. It had the ominous overtone of Bach's organs. It had the intensity of a witch's nine-inch-long nails scraping the surface of a grim blackboard, with the promise of pain. It rang in my apartment on my bedside table. The radio switched on automatically too. Yuppie-friendly gadgetry to get your ass on its way to more cheese, in style. I rubbed my face, seriously contemplating the necessity of what I was about to do, again.

We had an old-looking apartment, decrepit and minimalist. A slightly scuffed sofa, a sturdy table with a couple of chairs, an old television, that was our drawing room. It was clean and quiet, ready for parental inspection in less than five minutes. This was supposed to be our temporary place before we adopted the joyous condo life of the undeservingly-rich-and-dying-to-be-famous. The morning light fell on our pale yellow walls and the ill-shaped drawing room spotlight grew.

I could smell the morning rain. Another muggy June day pushing me to stay in bed, inactive, incapacitated.

But alas, 'condominium coolness', wealth and joy come not easily to the lazy. I reached for the clock and slammed the damn thing down hard, staring into my empty balcony. My dying plant, a crow on the electricity lines criss-crossing the sky, a view of the building across the road—sights seen every day, like clockwork, like the insides of a machine. The plant had been a gift from my sarcastic friend Shahnaz. She told me I 'needed some green in my life'. Look at it now. Yellow and dry. Even the birds in our neighbourhood seemed to work on schedules and appointments. Who could blame the poor things? Routine ruled us all. Well, most of us.

Lying on the dishevelled bed with crumpled sheets and pillows strewn all over the place, evidence of another night spent tossing and turning, I traced the slowly moving blades of the fan. I suppose after you've been beaten into a mould long enough, you start asking whether you deserve any better. I was close to entering into my own sickly comfort zone, loathing myself for sometimes believing that what I had might just be it. I felt like a horrible tool. Dreams of achievement, dreams of changing all that's wrong had been replaced by drab Excel spreadsheets with macros to boot. My personal island of torture. How could I possibly spend more years like this and 'grow within the business' to be a clown like my boss? Selling bullshit for top dollar and smiling through the ignominy of being a hopeless sell-out myself. How could that make anyone feel even remotely content? I rubbed my eyes to fully wake up.

'Live better,' signed-off the annoying bubblegum announcer on my radio. I kicked it to a stop and punched in some Queens of the Stone Age. A lot of the time music provided me with an escape. It was my numbing agent, delivering peace, shifting focus: anaesthesia for the day's surgical assault on my self-esteem and soul.

'I am not condemned . . . no this is not a chore . . . I am not condemned . . .'

Musically inspired auto suggestions for peace and calm too proved to be just temporary. The walk to the bathroom was slow and pronounced. The music was loud. Josh Homme insisted that I had a 'Monster in my Parasol'. I wish the song was about that. My monster was in my head. I decided to smoke it out. Not by means of a massive self-immolation bid, of course. I merely popped in my morning ciggy.

I wondered about the millions of pathetic clowns in a million houses getting ready just as I was. Digging through a lame wardrobe of weather-beaten white shirts, grey and black pants, yellow ties, smoking that first morning cigarette to get the day started. I saw the same sorry sight again.

I finished with my ablutions and made my way to the front door through the common area, fixing my tie knot. Ties were a must for days that we met clients.

Abhay, my housemate, had already picked up the papers delivered to our doorstep.

'Oye, have you seen my paper?'

'One sec, sorry da, picked up yours with mine.'

Abhay had a distinct liking for *Today's News*. I liked *News Today*. We sat at the table reading with a cup of tea and some lightly buttered toast. I continued my bid to delay myself, buttering and rebuttering my toast till Abhay snapped at me. 'Want me to inject it directly into your arteries?' he asked. I stared at him and dead panned, 'I need the lubrication.'

Abhay was the kind of guy who could be happy pretty much anywhere. He had given up any aspirations he might have had of being a world-beating reformer, his idealism had transformed into a dull daily ache that he was learning to ignore. We had studied together in college. We had been room-mates for two years there. He was a good guy, an ideal son and a reliable friend who had always tried his best to keep me out of trouble. He was my lanky Tamilian housemate in search of his mother's daughter-in-law.

I didn't want to be where he was though, in that state of acceptance. I still saw plenty that was wrong. I still felt the need to hit out at the powers that be, which had put me where I was. The well-oiled machine that had fooled me into 'gaining' all that I had.

In any case, he was a fairly successful chemical engineer. He knew his job and did it reasonably well. I had made a switch. I got bored of the engineering curriculum and took up an advertising and marketing job with a renowned firm.

Trouble is the conformist coward in me. Twenty years of doing 'the right thing', doing 'well', building my life, getting that condo, getting that car, pleasing my parents and my loved ones, that was the sum of my life. Responsibility to one's immediate family and managing their expectations has always been a priority. It is so for a lot of us and clearly this is where I get defensive.

Even the great Houdini would have had a hard time pleasing audiences today. Everyone's an escape artist, building illusions for themselves, building alternative realities where they're heroes. Distributing opportunities becomes a euphemism for keeping poor people in debt by lending them some more. Garnishing the details becomes a delicate way of saying 'we're going to lie our asses off and smile'. It could wring your neck or pound on your soul. It could gnaw at your insides, like a million murderous maggots were being poured into your bloodstream for a delightful serving at an abominable feast.

You're it, though. You're the hapless serving hurriedly venturing out of your apartment at 7.35 a.m. to reach your fantabulous office by 8.29 a.m. I turned to Abhay and said in my fakest television presenter voice, 'Have a great day at work!' He laughed sardonically and with a smile on his face, pointing with his right hand, said, 'You too!' For a moment we were easily excitable pre-pubescent VJs from the 'music' channels.

I followed him out of the apartment and down the stairs. We stood on the pavement in front of our building. I was imagining the tedious walk ahead. The rain had stopped and minor puddles marked the street. I pulled out my pack of cigarettes despondently. It was like our own little *Matrix* moment that has been overplayed and poorly replicated by numerous artists after the original. It's a telling instant when everything ceases, does a neat 360 and you grit your teeth at the end of it, because nothing has changed. The emptiness still looms large, the dung by your feet is still there, and you're still slowly poisoning your lungs. You're just a little more aware of everything. There's no leather-clad deep kick flying outwards. Not yet. Not quite yet.

I walked towards my office. The feeble walls on the side of the pavement had cracks in them. I could see faces in each of them, bricks with character grudgingly holding up structures that were housing the quiescent. People walked by me, faceless people with a purpose. Don't get me wrong; I judge us not for what we do for a living. I judge us for our state of oblivion, people expecting and accepting lies and bullshit. It's heartbreaking. This is not what we were meant to be. We're capable of so much more. I believe that. I know that.

The fruit seller on the roadside sat looking at his diseased wares. I guess the rain and poor shipping had damaged some of them. He stared unseeingly at the grapes and oranges before him willing them, I think, to become fresh and whole. Seeing a large crowd approaching he suddenly came alive. He began a long rant about his fruits. Short of grabbing people and force-feeding them the fruit, he did everything he could to fill polythene packets with parts of the pyramids before him and palm them off.

The moment you look at an ordinary fruit seller in the middle of the road and think of him as a metaphor for what you're getting in life, you know you have to do something about it.

I walked on.

It wasn't that I didn't express my anger, my thoughts on what was wrong. Abhay and I discussed politics, ethics and what we're here to do all the time. Our levels of desperation used to range from 'Somebody's got to beat the shit out of that guy for anyone to learn anything' to 'I wish I was there, making policy, shaping opinions'.

Sure we'd seen the movies where some fresh-faced kid takes things into his own hands, destroys the evil political party, gets the girl, beats up gangs of miscreants and kills Amrish Puri. Sometimes we were quite convinced that Sunny Deol should really do that shit. At others we realized that it would never work and that violence was not the way to fix things. Violence loses you the all-important moral high ground. It fucks your credibility and leaves you in the ranks of common criminals.

Then there were the non-violent protests, candlelight vigils and marches. Good ways forward, but far too common and far too tame to have any impact on anyone for an extended period of time. We're all too jaded to be moved by a mass of people shouting slogans or lighting candles.

Sure we could start NGOs and work at the grass roots, without asking too many questions and encountering the establishment only when it was damn near necessary. That sounded good. That sounded appealing. But hell, to reach out to over a billion people and to reach out to them fast you had to make a statement. You had to capture their attention and their imagination. How the fuck does one do all that? That was the question that dogged me.

So, all my tirades and anxieties found their way into my essays. They weren't just scholastic ponderings of an angry kid. They were action statements with detailed descriptions of how to mess with whom. They were my voice. They gave me an outlet, and embodied my venom and pain. It was only a matter of time until the right stimulus came along: the thing that would push me over the proverbial edge, leading me into an abyss of my own creation, a dark tunnel with a 3W bulb flickering at the end. I didn't care. I'd choose a dying bulb over a blazing exit sign any day.

Sense by sense, I assimilated everything on my way again. I could see a potpourri of colours, the distinct stench of fresh sewage assaulted my nose and I heard the crass cacophony of a hoarse man screaming at another. They seemed to be colleagues. Perhaps accomplices would be a better word, given the nature of their conversation. I couldn't believe what I was hearing. I stood rapt in amazement, stunned by the unfolding conversation in the car idling at the traffic crossing.

'Why the fuck did you have to shoot him after I did?' barked the bigger man in the driver's seat. He was gritting his teeth and beating the steering wheel as he spoke. The other fellow sat guiltily beside him, looking down.

'He would have . . .' he whined.

'Did he?' It was a terrible inquest. Each question made the little man on the side shrink deeper into his seat. Passers-by could see that something was wrong between them but most just continued on their way. I was, for some reason, rooted to the ground.

'He could have . . .'

'Skill-less, loud-mouthed asshole!'

'He was shaking like an auto, I thought he was going for his gun . . .'

'That's what always happens! You didn't have to shoot him

in the head after that! How many times have I finished the job with a clean shot to the chest? How many times has anyone recovered from that?'

'Never . . .' came the uncomfortable reply.

'Ended up mopping the bloody place. Do I look like a fucking janitor to you?'

'I've never seen so much blood in my life either, I think for fat guys we should limit the bullets to a maximum of one . . .'

'Don't change the fucking subject . . . Today you messed up . . .'

All this while I stood by their rusting Fiat, not realizing that the light had changed and I could cross the road. Then the big guy stuck his head out of the window and started announcing to people in the street, 'Meet Anand Sarkar, everybody! The man who shoots the dead, ruins the living and is slowly putting Yamaraj out of business.'

'Basuji please, what is wrong with you? Please, please stop . . .' squealed the sidekick.

'He's the best in a long time, his aim would put the great Arjuna to shame, his resolve would make even Bhishma Pitamah weak . . .' Basu continued undeterred by Sarkar's yelps of indignation.

'I beg you, please stop . . . I won't do it ever again, Basuji!' Sarkar wheedled.

The pleading worked. Basu wriggled his torso back into the car.

'If you ever give me shit about how you're a slayer and this is what you're meant to do with your life, I will personally kick your sorry ass all the way back to Dhanbad, you fucking idiot!'

'I said . . . I know nothing else . . .'

'You know nothing. My hands are still stinking.'

Their argument continued. They must have done some other sucker in earlier. How could these guys be so unaffected by that? Sure, they were 'hard' hit men. Even I could see that. Raised on the street, shoplifted as kids, been beaten up and then beaten up people. Sure. And here I was uncomfortable with what I have to do for a living.

What about prostitutes? How do they convince themselves to do what they do? Times of difficulty drive us all to do things we don't want to.

Why should being a prostitute even be an option?

Why should being a hit man even be an option?

Why should being a marketing hotshot even be an option?

My ponderings about diverse and possibly reprehensible jobs were interrupted by the quick and loud snapping of two dirty red fingers.

'What the fuck are you looking at?' It was the big guy from the car, Basu.

I had a bad habit of sometimes getting lost in my thoughts and forgetting where I was, or what I was doing. As a child I had stood in corners for it, done the murgi. My most recent suspended animation moment had led to a long lecture from an irate female driver, about the importance of 'seeing where you are going' when you're in the street. Until then it had been a source of amusement. Never thought it would almost get me killed.

'What the fuck are you standing here and listening to?'

'He probably heard everything, Basuji . . .'

'Come here!' said Basu with a sense of ownership that I resented.

'Come here, you prick,' Sarkar, the ineffective sidekick reiterated, as if I hadn't heard his boss.

I didn't fear them. I knew that if shit happened, the nearest policeman was about a hundred metres away. I also knew that he weighed about a hundred kilos.

I walked to the side of the car with caution.

'What did you hear?'

'Nothing.'

'What were you looking at?'

'Nothing.' I replied with a half shrug.

He smirked and asked me coyly. 'Do I look like a bad man to you?'

'No, you look just fine.'

'That's right. He's your regular, honest to God, bona fide living saint: Basuji.'

'Why the fuck are you giving him names, Anand Sarkar from Dhanbad?' he retorted menacingly. The sidekick realized he could do nothing right that day and apologetically fell silent.

'I believe you,' I reassured them.

'You don't think otherwise, do you, tie-shirt?'

'No. No, I don't.'

'Saala Phattu!'

'He's just another insignificant tie-shirt . . . forget him Basuji.'

'Get the fuck out of my sight. If I see you looking our way again, I'll plug you right here.'

I backed away, chagrined and angry, primarily because the rabid and uncouth murderer was right. He had read me for what I was and written me off with even greater ease. I was a nothing. I was a glorious, meaningless observer incapable of doing anything to him.

I stared down at the asphalt. Should I step out, out of turn? Should I complete my ineptitude and end my misery with a generous dose of bus engine bustle in my face? No. I will bring their war to them. Some day I will.

The light changed.

Taunting cries of 'Bye tie-shirt!' were the last I heard from Basu and Sarkar, as the squabbling dynamic duo blew kisses at me and drove off. Should make a note of their names.

So it ended; my perfect morning walk that is. Leading me gently into my office, an awesome place where grand deals were struck between hawkish bigwigs; where superb minds were put to their best use, coming up with magnificent ideas to sell cold drinks and chocolates. I was 'home'.

I walked past my boss's office, with its ostentatious wall hangings dominated by a framed print of a Dali that he routinely referred to as a Vinci. Fucking yuppie jackass. Could be me in ten years, if I do nothing about my life actually. He was a nice guy at heart I suppose, just a tool of our times. Forcing numbers down our throats, re-enforcing deadlines and restating the obvious, interspersed by pep talks that belong only on syrupy Zee TV kids' shows of old.

'You belong!'

'There is something *special* about every one of you.'

'Tap into your potential.'

Well, I'm all tapped out, sir. And no, don't ask me for the Pegasus shorts.

'Pranav, where are the Pegasus shorts?' I heard him boom from behind me.

'I'll have them done by the afternoon, sir.' I exhaled.

'We have a presentation scheduled for them this afternoon. Have them ready by eleven. I know you can do it.'

I cut him off before his 'You're the idea man' speech could be recalled and regurgitated.

'I can't come up with a campaign for that stuff so easily.'

'You have to.'

'Let me see what I can do,' defeated, I said.

'See me in my office in ten minutes, I need to make a call or two before that. Pushpa will bring you in.' He smiled.

'Bring me my numbers,' he told his big-spectacled secretary. She flashed us with fake smile number thirteen from the Close-Up catalogue. I cringed. I cringed because for the past couple of months I had been doing the same thing, groping in my bag of tricks for the right smile. One that combined the right approving nod with just enough conviction and enthusiasm. My bag was empty. I had been brought up to respect what I do. I tried my best to get through the days, chipping away at the old block, trying to find my way.

I had spent time in many a meeting watching people's mouths move. It was my little malediction, to watch them rack up numbers on a chart and babble along while I struggled with my own personal 1929. I was sure they were making sense and being eloquent. It had become white noise to me. The fancy lingo and generic format for communication made it easy for me to respond appropriately and in a timely fashion. I would have responded 'correctly' if these people were all speaking Latin, German or Cantonese. The meetings and requirements were so well structured. Besides if you are even half listening you can say the right shit just by gauging the tone of the sentence someone throws out at you. Try it sometime.

I ambled over to my desk and switched on my computer. Some of the guys strolled past my desk without saying hello or good morning. I think people in my office were a little scared of me. Lately I had been putting them down more frequently. Their lunch conversations would bore me. They made me more acerbic. They made me see what I was and made me compare it to what I ought to be. Their unbridled positivity was anything but contagious. Vaibhav came over. He was a short chap, I could only see his eyes over the wall of my cubicle. His eyebrows danced as he told me how great a day it was to be at work. I looked at him blankly. He had just been given a compliment by the boss for his handling of the XS3000 account. They were new in India and were going to have a huge launch in a few weeks. He wanted me to share in his mini celebration as he handed me his project plan for kudos and criticism. I barely looked up at him. The dancing eyebrows gave one last exasperated bounce and disappeared.

I opened my email for the briefing documents. There it was, in front of me again. Pegasus.

Pegasus was a client that I would happily award to my worst enemies. They sold the most inane and irrelevant things. Things for which a lot of my friends would stand in line for hours in the rain, just to get a look. They say that is normal. Wanting a good life is *normal*. A good life being defined by the new Pegasus Flex Master 7007 leather chair with vibrating ass pads, arm massagers and neck cushions that'll make your mother weep when she sees how fucking successful you are. How fucking *normal!*

Often my friends had implored me to join them on their weekend self-improvement-through-retail jaunts. I told them that an ass in a hat was still an ass.

Normal meant stoking your ego with the latest television, hooking you up with crystal-clear information about quality merchandise that could make your life brighter, easier and indescribably more fulfilling. Normal meant being on a frequent-flyer programme that racked up points like a blitzkrieg, so that you can ride around in one of your Zeppelins to Barbados. Normal meant being on a frequent-flower programme with the most exorbitant and pretentious florist in town, to keep your demanding wife or girlfriend pleased enough to go to Barbados with you. Normal was death. Normal was oblivion. Normal was a painful pin reminding us that we're satisfied living for ourselves. Fuck normal.

Shahnaz called. She wanted to know how I was doing.

'I need to get out. I feel like writing. I feel like falling off the top of a building and writing on my way down, weightless, with the wind in my face, people in the windows watching me fall, some screaming, some in awe. The pen slips out of my hand, it doesn't go far, I reach for it and continue to write . . .' My free-falling ways met their abrupt, concrete end when Pushpa walked by and I thought my time had come.

'Tiny insignificant detail, this, but you usually use a laptop n'est ce pas? You really want to free-fall with your new expensive toy?' Shahnaz joked.

'No, initial notes are usually in longhand, but I could free fall with the toy too. Neither of us would make it, so there's no risk of heartache.'

Shahnaz laughed and disconnected with a cheery 'See you later'. Snapping my phone shut, I stood up for a moment and looked around at the people in the office.

Pushpa Brar in her push-up bra stands up from her desk and starts pacing up and down in front of it. On a slow day my mind usually takes flight. Everything else switches to autopilot and I walk through the day, knee-jerk responses and appropriate vocalizations save my ass and get me through. Pushpa is still pacing up and down in front of her desk. Like a human pendulum she hypnotizes me. I sit back down in my chair.

Atmospheric sounds of distant guitar twangs washed over me as I sat in fake alertness at my desk, typing away furiously. Asdfghjkl asdfghjkl poiuytrewq qwertyuiop. Perfect sense! Or should I say mnbvcxz zxcvbnm.

I waited at my desk, staring at the screen, asking myself another one of my favourite questions.

'Now what the fuck am I going to do?'

3. THANK YOU FOR THE COFFEE

It was as if there was no light, the office was nothing more than a dark hall, still and silent, holding its breath ominously. I sat waiting in my cubicle. Expecting the fluorescent panes above me to brighten my day and rid me of my gloom. It was a near-spiritual experience. It was a dream. I sat gaping into what was now a mirror. Like Buster Keaton, an uninspired and insipid reflection stared back at me. What was all that training for? What was all the hard work for? Years of preparation for something big, something worthwhile and fulfilling were ending in a despondent fizzle. I was frothing with ideas yet tied down by a system that was so smug and demented that I didn't know where to start.

Perhaps with the Pegasus shorts.

Pushpa Brar in her push-up bra slithered up behind me.

'Boss will see you now,' she cooed.

I rose from my chair and made my way to his office. He had stepped into the loo it seemed. I waited for a few minutes before the executive flush of the executive bathroom was executed and faintly heard. Those things were supposed to be practically inaudible. He stepped out drying his hands with a look of great concern on his face. It was as though he seemed to know something that was disturbing him and he was waiting for the right moment to share it with me. He seemed pensive, visibly searching for a way to start the conversation.

I thought I'd help him out and give everything a second shot.

Before I could say something inane about how impressive the view from his office was, how magnificently it encompassed the delicate architectural balance between modernity and tradition that is characteristic of Mumbai, my heart screamed for me to bite my tongue. This job was turning my anatomy on itself.

I remembered a recent lunch with him. We had gone down to the café with a few colleagues. We sat down at the usual table and looked at each other. Our boss had a big set of lunch boxes packed by his imaginative and creative wife's overworked and harried maid. He sat in front of me and looked at what I had. It was a small sandwich that I had just bought from the first stall at the corner. He looked at it with wanting eyes and then looked back up at me.

I said, 'Would you like a piece?'

He smiled and said, 'Thanks, I'll help myself.'

With that he reached across the table and made a large incision on the left side of my chest with his elaborate cutlery. He then proceeded to feel inside my chest for my fist-sized muscle and pulled it out. He bit into it and little bits squirted around at us all. No one reacted too much, it was impolite to do so.

'This is fantastic! Where did you get this?'

'Delhi, sir, it's from Delhi,' I whispered before I fell unconscious on my seventy-five-rupee sandwich.

Maybe that didn't really happen.

'Sit, Pranav, sit.'

'Thanks.'

He appeared agitated.

'How are you finding your projects these days?'

'They're okay,' I stated with a matter-of-fact nod.

'How about working with the new team?'

'It's been good.'

'You aren't having trouble getting along with them?' He was disappointed by my short answers.

'They're all right'.

'I see . . .' He looked down at his pen, and then stealthily towards me.

'What was it that you wanted to see me about? You seem ill at ease, sir.'

'The thing is, Pranav, I don't know what is bothering you and want to find out. I somehow get the impression that you're not . . . happy.'

The H-word, he hesitated to use it at first but then for lack of a better alternative, there it was. The H-word.

'Why do you say that?' I was intrigued and wanted to see where this was coming from. This was new.

'Well, I've noticed a sharp decline in the quality of your work. You're sluggish. You don't seem to take any joy in it any more.'

'That is perhaps true.' Yes Edison, twist your bulb and tell me more. Call Tesla, maybe the two of you can figure it out.

'We'd like you to be more prompt with your deadlines. It's been weeks since we had the last meeting to discuss the Pegasus shorts.'

I listened to him patiently.

'Now, I've tried to be like a mentor to you. I care about talented people like you. Quite frankly, you've been an asset to the firm. I have people calling me for beauty product ads just because of you! Because of what *you* did for the P&G guys. That was brilliant.'

'Thank you, sir,' I said, feeling sick.

'What's bothering you?'

'I just . . .'

This was it. His obvious and apprehensive line of questioning deserved to be answered with honesty. I didn't think I could continue with my charade any more. I was no longer convinced that I had to slowly saw off my limbs every day of my life to climb some ladder that would lead me to a great promised land, or promised floor in my case. One that came with enrichment, glory, respect and hope. Most of all, a sense of self-worth.

I could no longer be the whore.

'Tell me, Pranav, we haven't got all day.' Mild agitation marked his tone as he looked over my shoulder at Pushpa who had stuck her head in with some papers. He gestured violently, asking her to leave.

I looked down at the fancy carpet under our feet, then at the 'Vinci' on the wall.

'Look, if you can't tell me we won't be able to fix whatever is wrong. Things, as they are, are largely unacceptable, especially for a bright chap like you.'

Terse, rational threats garnished by hope-inducing praise. Sounded like a quote from page fourteen of the *Manage Your Morons* handbook. He must have the hardcover version.

I looked at him, then through him and I saw the Porus Towers behind his balding head. They looked like horns. Was he the devil? I doubt it. He was merely an instrument, a small-fry facilitator recruiting for the cause.

'I can't do it any more,' I said, shaking my head.

'What do you mean?' His response was calm. He seemed distinctly pleased with himself as he thought that I was opening up to him.

'I can't do this any more,' I repeated, coldly this time.

This was met with a look of glee in his eyes. He now thought he knew what the problem was and began on a boisterous declamation to set me right.

'Oh, everybody has bad phases! Writers call it writers' block, advertisers call it a dead-end day. Oh, it happens even to the best of us, as is evident from the fact that it is happening to you!'

'It's not that I can't write, sir. I'm just tired of what I am writing.'

He sat up in his chair and then sank back into it. He was getting impatient, I could see. He tapped his fingers on the arms of his chair and then stopped.

'You'll have to help me understand this.'

I was in, this was indeed it.

'I don't like what we do here and I can't sell a stupid cold drink like it's the cure for cancer any more. I can't sell things that mean nothing to anyone until they hear about them. It just doesn't do anything for me any more.'

A deathly silence followed. He squinted at me, and the lines on his forehead grew thicker as he prodded me more.

'Again, you'll have to help me understand this . . .'

'It's quite simple, sir. I thank you for your effort and openness but this is not what I was meant to do. I won't be able to convince myself that my life is worth anything if I continue here.'

'You were responsible for almost 15 per cent of our profits last year! That's massive, son!'

'I don't care about that! I can't be the 15 per cent guy living for numbers, bullshitting and juicing a system based on stoking the desires of people.'

'You've developed a conscience? Is that what this is?'

'I've always had a conscience, sir. I've just stress-tested my being and I refuse to take it any further.'

'How would anyone ever sell or buy anything without us? You're questioning the very basis of an economy! Retail is our bread.'

'A guy works his butt off all day and goes home. He has a meagre meal with his eager, demanding family and they all settle down around the television. Through this magical invention they're brought in contact with the latest cars, fashions, restaurants, services that rule *your* market. Film stars exemplify the way you want to look as well as the way you'd like others to look. This makes his family and him even more demanding and it drives them all to a greater state of unrest. We're stoking fat. We're building wants. We're making an entire generation adopt cellphones and motorbikes as their goals. We're to blame for discontentment. If we don't get them through the television, we always have papers, magazines and billboards . . .'

He was angry now. Tilting forward slightly, he raised his voice. 'I'll play your game. I'll humour your fascination with being a myopic commie. What is wrong if a guy wants something new for his wife and kids? If a cycle owner wants to move up and forward to own a new Maruti? What is wrong with defining your success with material goals?'

'Everything. People are doing everything for the wrong reasons. Worse still, people are doing wrong things for these reasons.'

'Who the hell are you to decide what the right reason for anyone else to do anything is?'

'I would much rather have a world where everyone is aware of the fact that your vehicle or shoes don't make you who you are. I'm sick of the consumer manifesto that we're pushing.'

'So what do you want to sell? Ideals? Love, perhaps? No one's buying that shit.'

'Now there's a thought.'

'So is this the part where you tell me that you're quitting and moving to the Himalayas?'

'I am quitting, Mr Khanna. But I don't need to flee to the Himalayas. My Everest is right here.'

'You're making a big mistake. I don't see a fire for you to put out or run from.'

'I see a fire, sir. I see a whole generation burning. I loathe what I am when I spend hour after hour in here, scheming about the next assault on the populace. To sell what? Fucking sofas? Consumer debt is through the roof, people are living

way beyond their means for that sexy lifestyle, that piece-
of-shit vibrating sofa . . .'

'There is no need for that kind of language.'

'There is no need for that sofa. There is no need for that
condo, your fucking TAG and your cream Lexus.'

Now I had really pushed his buttons. I had just made
something that had been vague and ill-defined, personal and
pointed.

'Those things make me happy. They give me a well-
deserved sense of pride and importance. I will not listen to
you demean me in my own office.'

'Very well. But answer me this, which of these things do
you value yourself. What made you value your car or your
watch? Where did your perception of value come from?'

'From working my ass off every day for fifteen years, before
I could get those things. How dare you mock me?'

'Our entire value system is fucked up. Right from the start
we've got a propaganda going. Things matter, brands matter,
you've got to have the right stuff, from pin codes to pinstripes,
to be considered successful, to be seen as happy. I reject this
philosophy. Thanks for all the free coffee. I'm finally up.
Goodbye, sir.'

'Goodbye, Pranav.' The man was now trembling with rage.

As I marched out of his room, I was just glad he didn't try
sending me to that quack psychiatrist in Bandra who
recommends 'free laughter' and 'hourly smiling' as solutions
to a life of banality. A couple of guys from the office were
regulars with him. Wonder if they got a group discount or
something. Poor bastards.

After clearing my desk, I stepped out of the office with all that I wanted to take with me. Everything seemed beautiful again. An enormous weight had been lifted off my shoulders. I felt like the Pranav my school friends knew. I felt like the kid that everyone expected to shake the earth and squeeze it. I wanted to wreak havoc on this filthy system that tells us what to aspire for, tells us what to be, tells us what to respect. I wanted to make a statement. I wanted to be the Anarchist who saves us. I could almost hear my man Eddie Vedder singing 'Life Wasted' behind me, spurring me on.

'I'm never coming back again.'

The engineer-poet-jinglewriter was on his way home. Finally.

4. IF ROADSIDES WERE BEACHES

The only remnant now of my career as a tool of the advertising industry was the box I was carrying. It had stationery in it, some sketches and a long list of things I had been preparing for ages. I looked down at my little symbols of oppression. It was not easy to come to terms with the step that I had just taken. Everything was going to change. Everything was delightfully uncertain again. I trembled. A fresh breath of diesel was all I needed to bring me back to my senses.

I chose to enjoy my moment of freedom. In my strut of defiance I remembered my first interview ever. It was with an electronics manufacturing company. I recalled the interviewer's response when I told him that I thought his work was boring. I thought of all the opportunities that I had been given, as a student and even as an adman. Nothing quite excited me. Motivation had been really hard to come by. Not this time though. Not ever again.

My reverie was interrupted by a sight that made me burn with rage. There was a huge billboard pasted low, by the sidewalk. It had the picture of some famous model's famous rear. She was wearing nothing but a string of diamonds. The background was kohl black and only her body with the diamonds on it was lit. It glowed in the afternoon sun like a bush on fire. The gothic caption read:

Drape her in stars.
She deserves nothing less.
E.N.V. Diamonds

In front of this monstrosity there was a little boy, not more than eight years old. He was in tattered clothes, skipping along with a slingshot in his hand. He was coming towards me. I smiled to myself, seeing how happy he was. I stepped playfully from side to side to stop him. He looked at me in mock anger, nose goo dripping from his tiny nostrils. The grand canyon of disparities lay before me.

'What's the matter?' he snapped, his eyes bright and curious.

'Nothing,' I said. 'Heading off to school?'

He rubbed the grey-green refuse off his face and wiped it on his shirt. Lifting his slingshot up and aiming for my face he said:

'Mazaak karta hai kya?'

I raised my right hand in surrender, almost losing control of the box. The slingshot was lowered and no one was hurt. The crisis had been averted. I felt bad and let the young gentleman pass.

I wanted to tell him to go to school, but didn't. What good would it be? The poor chap would study, get a job and then work the rest of his life trying to afford those stones from the billboard. I had heard the kids in the street talk about the cars they wanted to buy, the big houses and the lush farms. Why are our dreams always dollar green in colour? Why does a child of seven want to be driven around in a Mercedes instead of an Esteem? Is it fundamentally wrong to dream of doing 'well'? I guess not. I am no one to tell a person who has had to struggle all his life that he shouldn't enjoy the basic things that he can enjoy. I have the luxury of my thoughts because I don't have to worry about two square meals a day, a decent home, money in the bank. But should greed be the motivation for any kind of activity? Should lust be the driver? This greed and this very lust that we fuel from the moment we know we are alive is the cause of all our problems. It is the cause of corruption and crime. As long as you want, you can never be happy. That of course is the biggest goof of all time. Most of us know precisely what we want to do with our next three salaries, largely thanks to sad fuckers like me.

Why do people like diamonds? Why is commitment in a romantic relationship not considered serious unless its sealed with a diamond ring? If you don't get the girl you love a diamond ring, do you love her any less?

In a state where pop satisfaction is everyone's immediate goal, what we value today is increasingly defined by a series of biases that we've been fed by the system.

The system is your parents, your government, your television and your goddam radio. Anything and everything has been a part of this brainwashing campaign where we've all been taught to value 'things'. The kid in the street has access to the system too and he's learning fast.

Your brother in the States is successful if he just bought a new car. Your government is doing well if it just got the approval of some other fuck all nation's lunatic leader. Your day was improved by the fact that you could use a coupon at your favourite designer coffee shop, all because you're a preferred customer. Your girlfriend loves you more for spending a couple of thousand extra on a necklace for her, because giving a necklace shows that you care. Valuing things implies valuing people. A beautiful scam.

What about real value? What about everything that would be left if we took away the house, car, business card, cell-phone, monogrammed Italian silk pyjamas and the electric toothbrush? What would you be? What's inside you? What drives you other than the false sense of superiority and satisfaction that you get from material goods and lame pats on the back that mean nothing?

We've been blinded by the propaganda. We're consumers first and humans later.

We're in a society where people consider it legitimate to sell their bodies and souls for a shot at the 'good' life. It is all seen as a suitable means to get what you think you deserve. We've polished human desires and fired imaginations to the extent that each and every one of us has an elaborate fantasy to fulfil. Little do we realize that we don't need much to be happy. We don't realize or appreciate how much we already have in pursuit of things we may never find. Often things that we want to afford.

'You're doing well for yourself, Pranav. You too, Abhay. We're proud of you.' His proud mother claimed.

'Yes Amma, see we got this new couch. Nothing beats watching a match on this thing.'

'He's right, Aunty, it has the most perfect ass-indentation for the young Indian male.'

Human desires defined and chiselled to perfection.

The spring in my step was back.

I got to my place, put the box and bag aside and went straight for the fridge. I thought a 1.15 p.m. beer would be a good idea, a nice way to mark my newly acquired state of unemployment.

My flat looked so different, so new to me. Never had I seen it in the afternoon on a weekday before. Damn, so this is what it feels like! A quitter at home with all the cares of the world on his mind, I listened intently for something to break the monotony of the silence. There was nothing. It was eerie.

I sat sipping quietly, staring out at the main road. Pondering about what I should do. A lot of my time, I found, had been spent just as a spectator. Fortunately, the whole 'monkey see, monkey do' adage had failed for me. I watched the Kingfisher disappear. Then I got another.

I wandered around the apartment gathering all my papers, sketches and essays. I no longer felt ashamed to read my own work. I felt that the hypocrisy had passed.

Printouts, handwritten speeches, rants in my notebooks; I read them all, scattering papers as I worked through the thick stack. The bricolage grew. It was like a beautiful cloudy sky, patches of white here and there with an occasional splatter of paint. I sat before it, looking for my answers. Imagining what my course of action would be. I started making two piles: 'Publishable' and 'Not'.

So far none of my work had made it anywhere outside my school and college publications. This, of course, had not deterred me from writing, ever.

Another trip to the publishers' was in store for me, I thought. There was no time to waste. I had spoken to a few people about this before. I had to delve deep into my stash for a solution. The earlier attempts had all been discouraging. 'I hope you weren't counting on this working out for you' and other such clichés were all I received. They thought that a guy like me didn't have a chance. They thought I preached too much through my writing. They were right. Some of them even laughed. All I ever heard was 'No', from people who had come to hate my guts, perhaps because I was a little too persistent. I was unsure of whether I had it in me to go through that again. Was it truly the way for me? To be heard and to have an impact, I thought my ideas needed a bigger canvas.

I started thinking about how people get heard. I started seeing how hopeless the existing channels of communication were.

Another beer went down. I read and reread the pieces. I laid them out all over the floor, short of pasting them on the walls. Lying back on them, I picked up piece after piece for inspection.

'What are those guys going to see in this?'

'Who's going to ride your wild horses?' Monsieur Bono asked in his earnest voice.

Beer number four. I paced up and down the drawing room. We had a tall oval mirror in front of the main entrance. I stopped in front of it, thinking. Looking at myself . . .

'Should you be the crazy guy distributing fliers at the train station? Who's going to hear you then, huh? 'the fuck's the matter with you?'

For some reason the mirror spoke with a New York Italian accent. Too much Scorsese I presumed.

There had to be rock star publicity tied up with a strong message. It had to be the kind of message you couldn't ignore.

Five beers down and my six-pack was fast disappearing. I walked to my desk and held on to the chair. The room seemed a little wavy now, moving in fits and starts. Fortunately, the turmoil was only on the outside. For, in my mind everything was clear. I had discovered my path. I had the confidence and belief that can come only after downing almost three litres of beer.

I sat down and reached for a pen. I laughed out loud. Shivering, I pulled a blank A4 towards myself and wrote these words on the top of the page:

The Anarchist Project
by
Pranav Kumar

The wall in front of my desk had never seemed so beautiful. Gentle cracks reached desperately for the ceiling. The dull light from my lamp caressing them, as though it were trying to pull them down. These cracks are going places. These cracks are going to touch the ceiling.

With that thought I fell asleep right there. At my table.

5. REVERIE

In my slumber things that I had abandoned and locked away as memorable moments from someone else's life now came back to me as my own dreams. I thought of Shahnaz and her shenanigans.

We had always been a little different from our other friends, Shahnaz and I. She wrote a lot too. With enviable regularity she would articulate my opinions and thoughts in a way that I couldn't. This was a girl who was reading Chomsky at fourteen while her friends grappled with *Sweet Valley High* and the like. Then there was her long Ayn Rand phase or to be more precise: her long *The Fountainhead* phase. She'd talk passionately about Howard Roark and then she'd sigh unhappily, lamenting that 'he was impossible'. Her dad was an architect and he'd laugh at her illusions about Howard. She'd get upset and call me. We'd talk at length about things she had read or about what was in the papers. She kept a little scrapbook of events that moved her. I started contributing to it too, and with time it grew. We had our own little journal of influences and opinions. We knew all the stands and most of the arguments. We became outcasts in our homes for being 'depressive'. The morbid fascination with taking everything personally can be trying for even the most patient parent.

I remember when she came to my house once after a fight with her father. We had been in the last year of school. Shahnaz's family had been neck-deep in wedding preparations; her sister Sarah was to be married that weekend. In the midst of all the last-minute preparations and excitement, Shahnaz had made the ridiculous demand that she be allowed to go and volunteer at a nearby village where people were dying because of a famine caused by drought. Needless to say, there had been a lot of tension at home.

'If you won't let me go, at least scale it down, Pa, scale it all down. Let's not do this. People are dying of hunger and thirst not fifty kilometres from here and here we are having this lavish wedding. It's not right. You know that . . .' she had pleaded, outraged at how unaffected everyone seemed by the unfolding tragedy.

But her father had been firm. 'Our lives have to go on, Shahnaz, regardless of what's happening out there. It is not our problem, child! You must learn to live with the sadness that surrounds you. You can be affected by these events. In fact, you should be. You're a sensitive young girl and I'm proud of you. But you have to understand that this is an important and auspicious occasion for the family . . . we have to make the best of it.'

That was when she walked out. Taking a beating and being handed consolation prizes was common for me and her. She came to my place looking for me to share her disbelief at how unmoved her family was. I tried.

I believe we're all born revolutionaries, with clear ideas of right and wrong; things are put into black and white for us by parents, uncles, aunties and the rest of the village that raises a child. It's when you hit adolescence that things begin to change. Those early teenage years when disparities eat into you and you feel like a communist: self-righteous, well meaning and easily angered. And then you segue into your lusting late teens, when you feel like a capitalist of sorts. You feel like you can and should *get what you think you deserve*. You feel people can and should fend for themselves. You hit the ultimate stage of this cycle after a few years of work, when you're a few years away from thirty. That's when you become a cynic, a pseudo-pacifist, not easily moved, not affected by anyone but yourself, looking out for no one else but yourself.

I was sick of being told that we were just kids whenever we would clash with our parents. We were supposed to get carried away it seemed. Nodding understandingly, they told us we'd outgrow it. However, some of us, in this crude life cycle, refused to grow up.

Well, to a certain extent we did. We were still affected by the disparities around us. The outrage still existed. Somehow though, it never translated into anything beyond a sour discussion. We had become the people we hated: loud, opinionated, compulsive coffee-drinkers with a lot to say but nothing to offer in the form of action.

I remember standing in my little veranda, watching her walk down the lane towards my house: an angry, quiet and hurt spot of clarity on the otherwise blurry streets. She stood at the gate and looked me in the eye. When I walked to the gate, concerned, she calmed herself to say this to me, her eyes bright with welling tears:

'We need to get out of here or change this place.'

6. THE FIRST ALTERNATIVE

The agitated fluttering woke me up. Squawks of desperation echoed in my head as I tried to regain my senses. A pigeon was trapped inside my room. It was flying about, bumping into the large panes of the glass door, the cupboard and, of course, the windows, trying to exit the way it had entered. As I sat groggily watching the pigeon fly about, Abhay ran in.

'What's going on?'

'There's a bird trapped inside.' I yawned.

'Damn, anyone trapped with you should be set free ASAP.'

'Well, hurry up then!' I played along.

He chuckled as he opened the windows with a great heave. We watched the little pigeon as she figured out what had just happened. Abhay stood expectantly over her, waving his arms towards the gaping exit. Our chirping companion seemed confused at first and she approached the opening with caution.

'Go on, now!' exclaimed Abhay. She fluttered once more and then with the flap of a wing was out on her way to freedom again.

'Well, that was an ordeal. I hope it didn't injure itself bumping around in this place,' I said.

'Forget it! She's fine,' he said while walking out of the room. 'I'm cooking rice and sambhar. Get ready for the greatest combination of herbs you've ever tasted.'

'Sounds good. Man, you're like a female Sanjeev Kapoor,' I teased as I stretched and stood. 'When did you get home? I never realized you were back.'

'Just about an hour ago. What time did you get back?'

I walked away towards the loo. I knew there'd be a loud response to my next statement.

'I've been here since 1.15. I quit today.'

That was enough for him to launch off into a furious avalanche of questions and imprecations. I shut the door promptly.

'We'll talk about this when I get out, I'd like to pee in peace,' I said from inside.

An hour had passed. The dal and rice sat uncooked, soaking in water. Abhay sat stupefied.

'This is not going to be easy,' he said with a sense of profundity and deep concern.

'Not for anyone,' I agreed.

'What are your parents going to say?'

I thought this was uncharacteristically delayed, even for an afterthought, coming from Abhay.

'I'll handle them, I'll tell them I'm looking for something else.'

'Will this "something else" pay the rent?'

'I have a decent stash to tide me through for a while. Don't worry about rent.'

'Tell me once again why you did this?'

'I couldn't take it any more, man. That's all. Not going to be a tool.'

'I see,' he said thoughtfully. 'So I'm a tool?'

'No, you aren't directly pumping the system with fuel. You're just a minion, a victim at best.'

'Good to know,' he mocked me. 'So what are you going to do?'

'Change is in order. I want to be the agent.'

'That's a lot clearer, Plato. Care to quit talking in riddles and clarify for the Republic?'

'I've got plans. I'm going to get published. I'm going to talk about things that people have stopped thinking about today. I want to demonstrate how we're all becoming machines chasing material goods and pop satisfaction.'

He seemed rattled.

'You know how those jaunts to the publishers end. Have you got new stuff?'

'I'm packaging my writing in a new way. Might work.'

He got up and walked to the kitchen.

'It's your choice, giving up a perfectly good, high-paying job to be pushed around by publishers who hate you.' He had done this speech before. 'I know how you worked your way up, man, it's not easy to get where you were.'

'We'll see . . .'

There was a brief silence.

'You don't seem to be cooking any more,' I said with a smile.

He was holding the pot in his hand and staring intently at the rice. He looked back at me.

'Wanna get some dosas in the system?' he asked, giving up on the sambhar-rice plan.

'Sure, let's go.'

He loved this little place round the block that he claimed served authentic south Indian food that wasn't adulterated for the north Indian palate. It was good stuff.

We talked some more through dinner. Discussing a long list of diverse unrelated incidents from days long gone. The night ended in laughter, a light drizzle and the lonely crooning of our neighbourhood paanwallah's radio.

I went to bed early. Tomorrow was going to be an important day.

7. THE PUBLISHERS

It was a clean-looking office. The reception was well lit and surprisingly packed for a Wednesday afternoon. Some of the people waiting in the hall had manuscripts clutched in their hands. We were all waiting for some kind of light to shine through, and be seen and heard above the crowd. It hadn't happened for me till now. But I was still hopeful. This was my fourth office today. I was hungry. I was a little tired. I looked down at the floor, resting till my turn came. An editor at a publishing house I had approached earlier in the day had directed me to this publisher. I had read about this place in the paper. It was one of the few small publishing houses that accepted unsolicited work. They preferred to be approached via email. But from the looks of the aspiring authors sitting in the hall, they sometimes bent the rules. I had called the office an hour ago to set up a meeting with Mr Malhotra, the editor I had been referred to. After much hemming and hawing about schedules being full, Mr Malhotra gave me fifteen minutes from his busy day.

'People will understand,' I told myself as I was called in for the meeting with Mr Malhotra.

I was led to a brightly lit but small meeting room with a

glass table and two chairs. I pulled a chair close to the table and sat down, going over my synopsis one last time while I waited for Mr Malhotra. A few minutes later the door opened, and he entered and sat down in the chair before me, without a word. He was clearly annoyed at having to meet me at such short notice. It was immediately apparent that he was only obliging me because of his friend who had referred me to him. Tersely he asked for a description of the work I was pitching. I had to make this gentleman of fifty see my point and explain why my book was going to be the 'next big thing'. He scratched his head peering through the sheets that I handed him and asked, 'What's the story?'

'Well, there isn't really a story, it's a compilation of essays and poems about our collective desperation and need to draw a line to differentiate between what matters in our lives and what shouldn't.'

As I heard myself talk I realized I sounded too well rehearsed.

'Really? Interesting. Can you tell me a little more?' he asked dryly.

'I've written about things that bother me. I've expressed my grief and anger towards problems like prostitution, consumerism, environmental issues and a general sense of apathy that I see as common today.'

He didn't look impressed. Maybe I was in the wrong place. Maybe there wasn't a right place.

'So it's more like a commentary as opposed to a story.'

'Yes, I suppose you could say that it's a commentary showing how we've all been moulded to think in a particular way.'

'Are you a social worker or a professor?'

'No, no I'm not.' I was a little confused.

Patronizingly he added, 'I was just wondering whether you had some background like a degree in sociology or maybe you've got field experience, maybe you've done something that would lend a greater degree of credibility to your theories and ideas.'

'I see,' I said. What the fuck?

'Tell you what, why don't you leave your essays with us and we'll get back to you.'

'Do you like the concept?'

'It's different in my opinion, but honestly I can't think of many people who would like to read this. Maybe if you tried publishing it in an academic paper or magazine it would work, but there are very few takers for this kind of stuff.'

'I see.'

'Don't get me wrong now. I am sure your ideas are fascinating, but no one is interested in reading this kind of writing. It just won't sell. Especially since you don't really have a locus standi. I mean, the question really is: who are you? Why should people take you seriously and why should they read about your ideas and theories for the world? What have you done? If I were you, I would work on trying to answer those questions convincingly. Anyway, I don't mean to be rude but I do have another appointment, so I have to go. It's been nice meeting you and good luck with your career as a writer,' he said and stood up, clearly indicating that the meeting was over. I thanked him and walked out of the room.

'That ended well,' I muttered. But even my sarcasm didn't work to cheer me up any more.

As I walked out of the office, the receptionist smiled kindly at me. My dejection grew. What was I thinking? What was I expecting to have changed since the last time I banged on their doors looking for an opportunity? My work had always been 'too niche', 'too amateur', 'without mass appeal'. I wasn't a name and if no one knew who I was, my thoughts weren't important.

I wished that an apple would fall for me. I wished that three life-defining visions would reveal themselves to me, completing me and showing me the way forward. I'd make do with two.

Give me something! Anything! I thought.

Newton and the Buddha were indeed lucky. Do common men have defining moments?

I put in a call to Abhay and told him that things were not working out on the writing front. He claimed that he had told me this would happen, he said that I should have expected nothing else. Even my parents had told me through my early years that what I wrote was largely commercially unviable.

'Fuck it.'

I got myself some filter coffee at the dosa place. It started raining mildly and pedestrians outside the restaurant started moving faster. The road in front of the place grew chaotic as the rain became more intense. Resting my chin on my hand, I watched the smoke from my cigarette hug the steel glass that I drank from before it disappeared into the humid air.

Puddles formed and tempers flared. I felt ill. Nothing was going to work out. No one was going to read my stuff. Ever.

I walked home and found the couch. In true loser fashion I reached for the remote to let the box speak. Somewhere amidst the commercials I fell asleep.

It was a darkened stage. I knew there were people watching. I looked around to see if there were others with me. There was no one to turn to. I stood confused, staring out into the nothingness before me. I heard a voice call out from the distance.

'Come on now, show Uncle how you recite your poem!'

I felt like I was three again, a child who had accidentally walked into a room full of adults being playfully coerced into performing for them by proud family members. This was a little different though.

The voice continued. It was a baritone, growing in strength, booming louder now.

'Dance! Dance! Dance!'

It was a compelling order. Out of fear I did a few steps of a Charlie Chaplin tap dance. I had the maudlin face and everything.

'More! Do more!'

'Who is out there?'

It was as though someone had let the sun in. An angry sun that had been waiting outside impatiently, growing hotter and increasing in rage. It had become vengeful and was out to blind us all. It was an enormous spotlight. The sound of the switch that had been flicked to turn it on still echoed in the arena. I stood there in its beam, covering my eyes and trying hard to see what was before me as I writhed in immense discomfort. It followed me when I ran around the stage to get rid of it. Soon I realized that the chase would end in my defeat. I fell to the floor of the stage and looked down.

'No more?' the voice enquired.

'Fuck you!' I shouted back in anger. I didn't want to remain an animal in this strange circus of blinding lights.

The voice grew hushed and sounded hurt this time.

'Fuck us? Surely you don't mean that, my boy . . .'

The lights came on again and right in front of me there stood a marching band, dressed in orange and white. Behind them sat an audience. We were all in an amphitheatre.

'We only want what's best for you!'

'Oh no . . .' I muttered at the thought of the inevitable and started to run.

The band started playing as they marched towards me, following me around as the spotlight did. They weren't as nimble as the spotlight was, but they frightened me more. I ended up getting swept up by them, much to my dismay. I rolled off trombones and bumped into tubas, I was mistaken for a bass drum. I tried to fight my way out of the throng but there were too many of them and they were too strong. I was like a reluctant rock star riding a human wave. They carried me. I kicked and screamed trying to break free. And then suddenly, we came to a halt. The band stopped playing. I clambered off them. With military precision, they backed away and started marking time.

'About turn!'

They turned and marched away.

I lay there in the dark watching them go off the stage. I felt that there was more though. I wanted desperately to wake up. I just couldn't.

Another bar of light clicked on, behind me this time. I saw my shadow before me. The light moved and my shadow shrank. I heard the crisp ominous steps of a man in boots walking behind me. I flipped around and there he was. A large man, stout and round, in a suit and a bowler hat. They were about to ruin Magritte for me. He held an apple in his hand. It was green. Was this going to be a lecture ensuring my obedience, instilling the need to march with the demented band?

No.

He moved the apple and revealed his face. It was Roshan Abbas, the game show king. Long before movie stars and box office gods had made the game show their realm, this man was the king. He was his usual smiling self. Only now I could see fangs when he smiled. He waved his hands with a flourish, pointing to his right. He then threw the green apple into the distance, it disappeared from the light, and went flying into the unknown.

'Ouch! Bastard!' a man shouted from beyond. The unknown became less so. It was a game show audience that started clapping and the house lights illuminated them in their excitement.

I stood up and leaned towards Roshan. 'What the fuck is going on?'

He spoke in a stentorian voice. 'You don't want to play fetch it seems.'

'I don't.'

'You ought to. There's a lot out there to fetch. Ladies and gentlemen, our participant is out of place! He doesn't want to play . . .'

The boos and awws sounded canned. They were tight and right on cue. He walked towards them.

'Everyone must play!' He turned to me and called me closer. I obliged. I felt like a moron in a cage with curious onlookers poking me with sticks to make me dance.

'Look now, you have three doors . . .'

We turned around. Glorious orange curtains spread wide and opened before my overawed eyes. My underwhelmed soul looked for exits. There were bouncers twice my size at each exit. Were they holding Kalashnikovs? I wondered disbelievingly.

Roshan pulled out a cigar and tried to light it a few times. Apparently his lighter was giving way.

'Unreliable piece of shit,' he exclaimed.

Immediately a man appeared, running out of the wings on the right side of the stage. He was on fire. This man was actually on fire. I stepped forward to see if I could help him out with the orange curtains, douse the flames a bit. He shrieked. Roshan pulled me back. He walked to the man on fire and nonchalantly bent forward, lighting his Cuban. He then kicked the man away, who ran off without a word.

'That was the last guy who refused to play. Pick a door, Pranav. Pick it now.'

That's when my eyes opened.

8. STEEL OUT OF A LIFE OF LARD

Hours went by as I sat in my balcony staring out at the street. The nightmare had struck me to the core. An aura of gloom cloaked me, grey clouds above, rusty grey gutters beneath. Even the kids playing on the roadside seemed listless and bored.

I had this recurring vision. I'd be sitting at my desk at work. The boss's secretary would slide up to me and say, 'We're ready for you.' I would then reach into the third or fourth drawer of my desk and pull out a little handgun. Next, I would press the gun to my temple and pull the trigger. Over and over again, I had the same vision, starting at different times in the story. Sometimes I would just be reaching for the gun, at others I'd be on my desk in a pool of blood, the fluorescent bulbs above me flickering. There's nothing more liberating than coming to terms with your own death. It empowered me and made me think that I could do anything. I wouldn't necessarily get away with it, but I would certainly make it happen.

I wanted to shout out to the people in front of me. I wanted them to know who I was. I wanted to talk to them in a language that they understood and appreciated, bringing them up to speed with all that was amiss.

The phone rang. It had been ringing incessantly since I had informed my parents about my unemployed state. I could bet it was my father calling. Again. Poor old man, he had called more than three times that day. He told me that he was disappointed and that he wanted me to get back on my feet again. All I could say was that I was 'fine'.

It continued to ring, loud and shrill, piercing through the apartment. I reached out to the receiver and lifted it, expecting another lecture on life and how I had angered and let down my parents, my boss, the IRS and my aunty in Pune.

'Mr Kumar?'

'Yes.'

'I'm calling from the office of Gupta & Sons Publishers; did you leave us your card earlier today?'

'Yes, yes I did.' A sense of hope rippled up my spine as I sat up straighter, holding the phone just a little tighter in my hand. I was trying to keep the hope out of my voice. Trying to be cool.

'Are you the guy who wanted to extend?'

'Err, no . . .'

'Wait . . .' he thought he had cupped the phone as he yelled across to his colleague.

I could hear angry cries of 'Hang up, hang up . . . you called the wrong number.'

And: static.

The call ended abruptly and with it died my last hope of getting published. There weren't many people that I knew who could have had such a bad day, careerwise.

I walked over to the couch and lay down on it again.

'How am I going to get the stuff out? How much am I going to rework it?' I asked myself aloud.

There were bundles of paper on the coffee table beside me. The evening breeze ruffled them desultorily as it blew threw the apartment.

Should I be a ranting madman sending out an endless stream of Letters to the Editor complaining about complacency and our state of constant neediness? Should I head out and start an NGO of my own? Working in slums with poor children, educating them and teaching them not to listen to the channels that are trying to gift them with goals?

It stared me in the face again. My hopelessness. My derision. What would the impact be? Who would I reach? Who do I want to reach?

Everybody, I thought, I want everyone to know. My essays lay before me. And suddenly I knew what I had to do. The blood coursing through my veins had never felt so warm. I had never been so aware of my own state of being alive.

I began a letter:

My billion-strong brothers and sisters, desire running deep, we're running for ourselves from ourselves. It hasn't been like this, no, not ever before; we're out on the streets, an entire generation's roar. This is my scream.

We have to change this place. It's not enough. Our lives as we see them now are not enough.

If I had my way, this place would be a lot like a Rage against the Machine concert. Thousands shouting, 'Fuck you, I won't do what you tell me!' That would indeed be precious. But it can't happen.

We need to wake up. Our struggles and trials, though similar, are lonely by nature. Oshos and Oprahs will tell you how to live better. Magazines will tell you where to go, what to buy and whose ass to kiss.

There should be an antithesis to all this. There must be a different and new voice.

There is hope but it's going to be a lonely battle. You have to fight it yourself.

Ancient cultures often involved rituals with men dressed in weird outfits brandishing spears and axes chanting loudly. Often these men would be dancing around fires. They shouted and sang, invoking action. They offered prayers, painted rocks, walked over hot coals to bring peace, rainfall and bumper harvests, whatever the need of their people might have been. They were high priests, witch doctors and learned leaders of the tribe. Their actions attempted to bring something gainful to their people. They aimed to teach and involve everyone.

We need something as basic as that today to rally people and get behind a movement which is in essence a personal one.

Some cultures in the past relied on a select few performing sacrifices before the eyes of their brethren. The spectators would feel the marrow of the activity, learn, grow and relate to it at a very individual level. The performance was grand. The performance was public.

We needed a monumental gesture that stands tall in the minds of men and women for years to come. We needed a Bugs Bunny piano scene, at the end of which Fudd doesn't die but certainly learns to respect the rabbit.

I now knew what to do. I had to take their war to them. For far too long had I been a part of the system. For far too long had I warmed and greased its hinges. I knew how it worked. I knew the oil that it ran on.

I will have my own 'brand' of protest: my own billboard with things that I have always wanted to say: messages that are important and needed today to balance the shit-storm that already exists.

I'm bringing dung, paint and chemicals.

This will be a new beginning. For me and for you.

9. REMEMBER WHEN THEORY MET ACTION?

Now think of a primate. Perhaps a fuzzy rust orangutan set in his monkey ways of conducting business. Our monkey subject is really special. He has the unique distinction of being brought up on pumpkin pies alone. Ever since he was a little tree-swinger, he's been brought up on a steady, tasty but ultimately deadly diet of pumpkin pies. He has a very limited history with bananas. If he were given one today, he may not accept it immediately. He may not like it at first. But he will know that such a fruit exists. He will learn a new flavour. If the introduction is done well enough, through an incident that will make an impression on him, he shall 'know' about the banana. He shall know what he was meant to eat.

All I want is for the monkey to know the banana. I can't force him to eat it forever. I can't make him believe that pumpkin pies are fundamentally bad for him. That's for him to understand. It has to be his decision. The poor chap just needs to see that life could be simpler. That all he needs is a fucking banana; and television, magazines, movies, parents, the government and all his friends have been fooling him with propaganda related to pumpkin pies. Perhaps I deviated a little with that last analogy.

It was a painful realization that my writing and ideas were largely boring, the way they had been packaged. For people to take notice and for there to be any action somebody had to provide a much-needed impetus.

Abhay walked in.

'What are you so pleased about?' There was a touch of disbelief in his voice.

'Nothing,' I answered as nonchalantly as I could.

'What happened? Did someone finally say they'd publish your work?'

'Not exactly.'

'Hmm . . . I suggest you start calling people to find another job.'

'I've got a job.'

'Well, that was fast! Fucking idiot came around in no time!'

How happy he was.

'I thought it'd be hard to get you back on track this time. Where are you working?'

'Oh, I'm going to be working for myself.'

'You're starting your own agency?'

'You could say that, in a way, yes.' I smiled.

'Cool. What are you going to call it?'

'I'm not quite sure yet.'

'How about "The Vector Ad Agency"?'

'Sounds too much like a front for a bad Bond villain.

Though we'd be happy to hear any more suggestions you might have in that cheese factory of a head you lug around.'

'Yes, I guess you're right. But hell, that's a side issue, this is great news. Can I help? Do you need anything? Initial funding to get you through the early bits?'

'No thanks, I have some pretty solid savings that I'm finally going to put to good use.'

'Sure. Sounds good.'

An undeniable sense of relief shone through his excited chatter. He was a good friend.

'I might need your help with some of the logistics though.'

'Not a problem. Anything you need, brother.'

'Okay! So first up. Where can I find a good nursery?'

'Nursery? You mean flowers and shit?'

'No. Just the shit. I need a few barrels of khaad. Come, let's find out.'

'Khaad?'

I got up and made for the door. He started walking behind me after what I can only imagine was a moment to come to terms with my apparent newfound interest in horticulture. Manure to be exact. Poor chap. He'd be in on it soon enough.

As we got into the car and made it round the first bend in front of the Hussain Barber Shop, my fidgeting friend couldn't help himself any more.

'What are you up to?'

'What?'

'You've got that look in your eyes.'

The man knew me too well. 'What look?' I exclaimed.

'Your naughty, wait-till-he-finds-out-what-I-did-with-his-girlfriend look ...'

'Hey! That was once. And it was a long time ago. I've grown up.'

'Sure you have. And that was your evil twin brother who pranked the hell out of Sudeep and Salil last week.'

'Those morons are too easy. I'm moving on to bigger things.'

A light drizzle was setting in. I didn't bother to switch on the wipers, as we were just a minute away from our destination: Salma Aunty's nursery. I'd heard about her in a long conversation with one of our neighbours. She had a lovely collection, I had been told.

'All right. What the fuck is up?'

'Will you relax? We're just going to buy a shit-load of khaad, that's all.'

'We live on the third floor. You've either got a massive secret orchid plantation in your cupboards or you've lost your mind.'

We stopped at a light. There was a huge board on the side, above a building with an advertisement for the SHB Automobile Company.

'It's not for me, Abhay. It's for them.'

I pointed to the billboard. He stared at me with even greater bewilderment, cursing under his breath.

10. INCEPTION

It took longer than I had expected. He was his chicken-shit self, even more so than usual. I had to endure hours of 'You can't do that!', 'You're out of your mind!', 'You'll get caught!'

But I wasn't deterred. I told him I needed his help. I told him it was necessary for me to go through with it. After some time it became 'We can't do that!', 'We're going to get caught!'

Good evening, buy-in.

This was the only way the ideas would get out. They were my life and I wanted for them to make it to the people. It was necessary. There was an urge to act. This was precisely what we had been talking about as kids, as university students not very long ago. This was my way out of my drudgery, my quotidian struggle to be a man of value.

'Self-worth? You're talking about self-worth?'

'Yeah. My life has to have a purpose. I've finally found it.'

'So did Batman, you lunatic, and he's a fucking comic book character.'

'So what?'

'So, ordinary everyday people do not have to shake the earth to feel like they're alive.'

'Most people don't need to feel alive. I want them to see that a lot of what they've submitted themselves to is premium quality bullshit,' I said as I inspected our recently acquired wares.

'For that you want to be a fucking vigilante? Some kind of maniac running around town vandalizing things?'

'I'm going to sell the ideas. That's all. And someone's got to shine a light on the dingy, dirty corners.'

'You're going to piss a lot of people off, you know that, right?'

'Yes. But think about how beautiful it would be. Think about how we'd see ourselves, for once, for what we really are. Think about the debate. Think about the rattle. This is basic, Abhay. I need your help.'

'Listen, the only reason I would be a part of your insane scheme would be to make sure that you don't get arrested, caught or killed.'

'Don't you see the reason for doing this?'

'To an extent yes. But . . .'

'This is what it's about Abhay. This is our chance to bring about a change. I'm not killing anyone. I'm like a terrorist who doesn't kill people.'

'Yes, you've traded in your AK-47 for a warm teddy bear, right?'

'Indeed. It's a warm teddy bear with an axe in his head and his eyes on fire, wearing an apron that says "Your TV is Wrong" . . . perhaps . . .'

He didn't have much to say to that. He just walked out of the house muttering, 'You've lost your mind, Pranav. This time you've really lost it.'

I looked down at the sacks of manure that we had lugged back from Salma Aunty's place. Twenty of them lay in a heap in our living room, piled up beside my pristine couch.

'How does one kill greed?' I voiced my thoughts out aloud as I settled myself on my couch with a pad and pencil. 'How does one sell the right stuff?'

I scribbled away on my pad for a few minutes. I stopped as I heard footsteps approach the door to the apartment.

It hadn't been long since he had left.

'So this is what you meant by the new ad agency?' he asked speculatively.

'You're back. Yes. This is what I was talking about.'

'All right. I'm in. This is totally crazy. But count me in.'

'Wow. Are you sure?'

'Yes.'

'What made you see the light?'

'It's more like what brought me over to the dark side.'

'Right, Anakin.'

'Yeah. I just want to see the look on their faces when it happens.'

'Whatever works for you. Excellent.'

'So have you thought it through?'

This was my favourite part. I always believed that content was key and it was up to us to deliver it well. The execution would matter only if the idea being presented had weight.

'I've got a few ideas.'

'Are we going to sign off?'

'We'll do more than that, Abhay. We'll do much more than that.'

From a very early age, I had been practising the art of covering for my follies. Not without good reason, of course. Usually I was compelled to do so in order to escape a beating or some other form of devious punishment that only a seasoned authority figure like a parent or a teacher could concoct. I was well used to the cat-and-mouse game. I was used to the thrill that came with knowing *more* or knowing *better*.

I remembered my first real brush with authority. It was a fake recess. It was time off that we had invented for ourselves. The vapid emptiness of the late afternoon, right before school finished for the day, had drained us. We couldn't sit in the classroom waiting endlessly for the bell to ring for the day. We longed to just loll around and play a bit, vegetate and talk. Of course, we were smart enough to do so far away from the main building that had teachers and custodians crawling out of the crevices in the walls. The school's main building was a dark, cold place where learning was imperative and wanderlust inevitable. This odd combination had given birth to the mass bunk. The teacher was nowhere to be found. He was a traveller himself, it seemed.

So with my friends and a motley group of other students

I wandered out into the playgrounds in search of entertainment. Shahnaz and the other girls were happily skipping rope. The rest of 4A lay scattered around the fields like lazy drops of pollen, looking for an idea. Our sky-gazing antics and cricket-related altercations were interrupted by the angry voice of our vice principal. Mr Singh was here. Mr Singh looked pissed. A towering presence, it was as though his shadow covered the entire football field. We were his herd now. He owned us for the rest of the day and many believed, for the rest of our lives. He rounded us up in Nazi fashion. I couldn't believe the submissive nature of my comrades in the mass bunk. We marched back to his office, through the hallways of the old school building. The line trembled. Passers-by shook their heads and made mock cross symbols saying prayers for a condemned lot. Some of the louder comedians were rounded up to join the pack. No one was laughing now.

Mr Singh's office, like most vice principals' rooms, had its fair share of enigma and folklore attached to it. Obviously, it was regarded as a place where no one wanted to be taken. Scarred seniors who had been inside for the wrong reasons, told tales of frighteningly thin canes. Apparently there was an entire collection of them adorning the walls of our stickler disciplinarian's chambers. He was believed to lose his mind in a fit of rage, lashing out at children in the prime of their mischievous young lives.

After a while Mr Singh fell silent, tired of ranting at us, it seemed. We could just feel his eyes sweeping across us like a spotlight, as we walked slowly. They said he had a room inside his room where he'd lock children up. It was empty and there were no windows. It was tiny and smelt of phenyl. Our seniors had choked while sharing these horrific tales with us. It wasn't acting. They were truly sickened by the memory.

'So this is what death row feels like.'

'Shut up!'

'My mom's going to kill me.'

'Who says you're ever going to see her again? Just keep your head down and do as he says.'

They warned us about how he would question us and make us feel horrible. After the questioning he'd get up from his chair and walk around in circles. Reminiscent of my favourite moment from the movie *Jaws*. I'll have to rethink that. The experience was never meant to be pleasant. My stomach felt weird and before I could share this with my comrades they piped up with similar symptoms. It must have been the fear.

We reached the office. The enormous teak door was shut.

We stopped right outside it.

'Single file, you maggots!'

We gave him what he wanted, as his shining grey safari suit needled its way through us. He opened his door and looked back at us with menace. I don't know if it was just me, but I saw a glint of happiness in his eyes. He went into his room and there was a tense silence in the ranks. Suddenly a struggle broke out at the head of the line; kids were fighting to be second, third . . . just not the first one in. The ruckus drew him out of the room.

'Stop moving about, you animals. Is this what you come

here to do? Have you got any idea how much your parents want for you to do well? Have you any idea how much your education is worth? Ingrates! Fools!'

He disappeared from sight after this brief rant. We had heard it all before in some form or the other. We heard his giant chair being pulled back. It creaked portentously against the floor.

'Come in. One at a time.'

This dramatic statement was punctuated by the sound of a rod or stick of some kind being clapped against his desk. No one moved. We were trapped it seemed. We were in a trance. Someone had to do something. If he wanted an obsequious drone, he was in for a surprise. There was only one thing to do.

I stepped out from the line.

'I said come in. I know you are in front, Amoldeep,' he sang.

Amol didn't look very good at this time. He was hyperventilating and being helped up only to be pushed in by Sid and Vineet. Who could blame the poor bastards? I walked passed them heroically.

'Tell my parents, I tried,' I turned to them and said. Decent last words for a fourth grader. They looked at me in shock. I knocked on the door and let myself in, turning back one last time to see my friends and their jaws on the floor. Shahnaz looked down, worried, pained . . . all at once. This concern, for some reason, made me feel a little better as I stuck my head inside the Vice Principal's dungeon.

'Pranav!' I heard my friends shout out to me.

Their voices were lost behind the teak door.

This was one of my first face-to-face meetings with authority. We were going to have a long and turbulent relationship I thought. In part I blame my parents.

'Question everyone, question everything' was a good motto but not one that won you many friends. At this point of time, I had to befriend or impress Mr Singh.

'Where's Amoldeep?' he barked.

I broke right into it. There was no time for procrastination or waiting for the opportune moment, I was there for a reason.

My Brahmastra was about to be used up. Like a bolt of lightning I ran to his desk and picked up his super-thin cane. I ran for the door as he howled behind me, chasing me like a salivating wolf strapped into a luge.

'Come back here, maggot! Where do you think you are running to? This is my school! This is my school!'

Sweat ran down my brow as I ran wildly, arms flailing, cane in hand.

I dodged the orderly who jumped in my path to halt my progress and almost pushed our English teacher Ms Nigam over in my lunatic dash for freedom. I slid under the indoor volleyball net and looked back for a moment. Mr Singh was catching up.

He kept shouting out for me to stop but I didn't. I ran to the one place I knew I had to go.

I reached the canteen.

Sure enough our elusive teacher, the traveller, Arvind sir, sat there watching dust chase dust, with a cup of tea in his hand. I ran up to him and stood behind his chair. He did not notice me. I looked to my left and saw Mr Singh panting down towards me. He was livid with anger and exertion.

'Pranav Kumar!' he bellowed.

I just stood behind the chair as Arvind sir got up. He looked at me and then at Mr Singh.

I stepped towards the red Vice Principal and handed him the cane. He looked at me in disbelief, as he took it back and then turned to the truant teacher.

'Arvind sir teaches us maths on Thursday afternoons. It's a double period,' I said in my most matter-of-fact manner. I then stepped back and waited for it to happen. I wanted Arvind sir to get caned. Adults don't get caned enough. Perhaps some of them should.

'Go back to your class, Pranav,' said Mr Singh thoughtfully. 'I will deal with you later.'

'Good afternoon sirs,' I nodded and walked away slowly, hiding a smile.

The single file line from outside Mr Singh's office had moved and become a blob of confused and angry children piled up inside a corridor, as they watched me walk back to join them. A small half smile slipped out to let them know that all was well.

'We have to go back to the classroom,' I declared.

That was my day in the sun. Shahnaz thought I was stupid but brave.

'I'm fine! Look at me, do I not look okay to you?' I insisted.

'Barely! And *you* didn't have to do that!'

'Who did?' I smiled.

Other people thanked and congratulated me. I had survived. I had done it to myself and made it out alive. From then on, my friends and classmates started consulting me and even asking me to speak for them in stickier situations. I was the only people's lawyer in 4A. An accidental Clarence Darrow.

After that it was smooth sailing. At eleven I had set Aunty Chopra's dogs free in the middle of the afternoon after tying a piece of meat to her shameless and cruel security guard's chair.

More recently, I had convinced Marketing that they had in fact spent three times their budget, just to prove a point about their lax tracking methods.

The perilous lifestyle, albeit small and contained, had taught me well.

I didn't have all the answers. I didn't have all the remedies for everything that was awry. Just a few beliefs, a few statements. I wished for them to be like pieces of art, created through chaos, born out of an irrepressible desire to wake people up. Public Service Announcements were passé; it was time for Public Service Enactments.

It was only fitting that I chose to sign off as 'the Anarchists'.

II. DUNG CITY

The day had come. Fidgeting and yet again muttering under his breath, Abhay joined me in what would soon become an occasion for revelry and merriment. We were on our way to Act One.

The Pirelli Towers had long been used by big companies for their roadshows, campaigns and product launches. There was a massive amphitheatre right in front of the building that seated all the dignitaries and the media; there was also a lot of place for throngs of onlookers to take in the proceedings that were held at the centre of it all. Any firm with a large enough budget would choose to sell their stuff from there. In my day I too had orchestrated and helped organize numerous such events for a couple of colas and electronic devices. The place was a huge hit. Just like today's SHB car launch party was going to be.

'The talk of the town.' Indeed.

I assured Abhay that everything would go as planned and that we would be out of there soon. It was going to be quite a job lugging those sacks of manure up to the top of the building. First, of course, we had to take care of the closed-circuit television feeds that were there all over the building. As planned, we crept into the service office and stole a couple of janitor's uniforms and caps from the store. We were now Mohan and Vallabh of the 'Evershine Custodian Services Company'. Proudly we marched out of the office, only to be stopped by a gentleman who insisted that we weren't doing our jobs properly.

'I think you missed a spot,' he sneered smugly, pointing at his office.

He had us clear out a section of his office; there was all kinds of trash in there, mostly old pizza cartons, empty soft drink bottles, crumpled paper and pens that had run dry. What a pig. We were diligent and did his bidding, losing some time. After we had done the job we made our way to the back of the building. We could hear the microphones being tested out in front at the amphitheatre.

'It's on,' I said to Abhay.

'I can hear it too,' he shot back. 'We have to get a move on.'

Preparations were under way out in front, sound systems were being tested, light-display sets and smoke machines were all being calibrated for the magnificent show. It was a spectacle designed to mesmerize the unsuspecting populace queuing up eagerly to watch it. There was going to be confetti, there were going to be speeches, dances and lots of eye-pleasing gyrations. There were also going to be a large number of celebrities present, especially the company's brand ambassador, Johnny C (Gyanendra Chaturvedi in real life), a famous Bollywood actor. It was a circus: a very driven and pointed circus.

They had lined four of their latest models as specimens in the centre of the amphitheatre. These 'gorgeous works of art' would be revealed during the course of the show with much fanfare. I couldn't wait for the fun to begin.

As they managed and mixed their music to make sure that they'd get Will Smith to implore people to 'get jiggy with it', we mixed the manure in buckets of water and vinegar on the terrace of the building. The funk was unbearable. Zeus could have smelt the stench all the way from his throne on Olympus. Sure enough, a lesser being, a constable, came by to see what was going on. We heard someone thump their way up the stairs. Struggling to cover the buckets with an old tarpaulin that was lying on the terrace, we pushed them near some open barrels of sand and some sacks of cement that looked like debris from a recent renovation programme in the building. As the door swung open, we just about managed to sneak out of sight and hide behind a pair of enormous water tanks. Watching from behind the tank we realized it was a cop and prayed that he wouldn't be too careful in his scrutiny of the terrace.

We could hear the thunderous applause as Johnny C strode on the stage. The crowd was mesmerized. I turned to Abhay to ask him if he had brought the pamphlets, but anticipating my anxiety he pointed to the bag under his arm. 'Good work,' I whispered.

'Can't leave it all up to your fat ass, now, can we?' he said self-importantly.

'Right, right . . . what would I do without you, man . . .' I quipped, rolling my eyes.

'Sarcasm makes for a one-man show, Pranav.'

'Okay. Fine. Sorry. Now shut the fuck up before the cop spots us and . . . ssssshhhhh he's coming this way.'

The portly policeman walked by, swinging his baton. His curiosity satisfied, his duty mostly done, he called someone on his walkie-talkie and stated that all was clear and peaceful; there was just a rotten stench of manure.

'God alone knows what they do at this place.' He grimaced and ambled off the terrace.

Things were heating up downstairs. We thanked our lucky stars for the constable's stupidity, locked the access to the roof and continued to mix the ingredients of our little cocktail.

There was a lot of hustle-bustle around the foyer as people arrived for the launch. Investors, esteemed politicians and guests (men in suits with great expressions of self-importance) were seated at the least distance from the podium, while stands of photographers were stationed to the left and right. A large group of people had assembled to watch the pitch and to get a glimpse of the new car, as well as Johnny C mouthing off on stage. He welcomed everyone to the launch and apologized for the delay in kicking off the event. He tried cracking several bad jokes about the weather, stating that the rains had put a stop to the proceedings. The sun had been up and blazing all day.

'Well it's going to rain soon buddy!'

That was Abhay, grinning as he stirred the mixture one last time. He was getting excited.

A man with a clipboard was going insane near the stage.

'Where are the flowers? Where the hell are the flowers! This is unacceptable!'

A large number of people ran in every direction after he briefed them all angrily.

The chaos ensued in the foreground: Johnny C's atrocious Warwick-meets-Washington-meets-Wadala accent didn't make things much better.

'All right everybody! Hold on to your seats, we're going to start this baby up right now.'

Confetti flew down from the skies above, a light brightened the podium, bringing it to life.

Johnny C began his trademark romp towards the centre of the stage in his signature sparkling white suit, medallion and top hat. A couple of kids in the crowd had the same costume on.

'Where are my ladies?' he exclaimed.

The audience cheered in anticipation, hooting teens and corporate has-beens rejoiced as their big evening began. An evening dedicated to a luxury car, so coveted and so admired even before the fucking thing had been seen by anyone. Funny thing was that across the road from the Pirelli Towers, there sat eager onlookers, common men and women who obviously could not be allowed entry to the event. They too were enthralled by the spectacle that had snubbed them, making a beeline to rooftops, climbing up lamp posts and peering into the distance for a glimpse of the chhamiyas as they made their way on to the stage.

They surrounded the actor-emcee of the moment and stared out with typical model look number eleven. This is the one where they tighten their jaws and purse their delicate pouty lips out. I believe they squinted their eyes a bit too. That brings out intensity. At least that's what Tyra Banks would have you believe.

Gyanendra aka Johnny started talking again. He rambled on and on about the significance of the show. As he said his bit, the women around him swayed as though they were in his control. With the end of each sentence they changed positions, shaking their posteriors suggestively.

'Ladies and gentlemen, welcome to the launch of the SHB XS3000! We have a great evening planned for you all; a glorious performance by our dance troupe to heat things up and then senior managers of SHB will introduce the new beauty to you all. After that we will have a short question-and-answer session for members of the press, followed by cocktails and light refreshments that will be served in the lobby of the wonderful Pirelli building behind us.'

The audience cheered.

'Hit me girls,' he said, his voice rising with each word.

With that, the thirty scantily clad girls began dancing, in a frenzy of smoke, glitter and psychedelic lighting. The smoke cleared a bit and they could be seen clutching on to Johnny C's arms and looking out into the crowd seductively. They started gyrating to some low-grade, old club music and then moved forward in a line, facing the audience in front of the stage, making gestures with their hands, throwing back their hair and twisting their tongues.

Proverbial dhikhchick sounds filled the atmosphere.

The idea, as I understand it, was to generate a heightened

degree of sexuality for the ad campaign, something one would naturally associate with a car. Elementary advertising.

They walked from one end of the stage to the other, playing with the audience now, smiling as they displayed their assets. Everybody cheered them on.

The thumping dhikhchick-dhikhchick was now followed by minor variations, like dhikhchicky. I marvelled at how they came up with that stuff.

The music died down a bit and the troupe chanted. They switched into cheerleading mode. Great torches marked the highlights of the performance; all we could make out from above was a light-and-smoke-induced mayhem, with colours that most nightclubs refrain from using.

You want it? You got it!
You never would've thought it,
XS three oh oh oh, do you want it?

The 'oh's were suspiciously elongated, a little pained and had a distinct evocation of pleasure associated with them. It was vomitous.

Abhay was checking the roof to make sure there weren't any other people there. No cameras either. He was humming his favourite Pearl Jam song as he did this. I thought it was quite appropriate:

The whole world will be different soon;
The whole world will be reliev-ed . . .

As the dance came to a close, the crowd grew louder and began their own kind of cheering. It made me sad to see that this was entertainment, made me sad to see that many actually enjoyed this.

It was time for Mr Big Shot himself, the cocky Mr Robin Kapoor, to take the stage. He was SHB's widely revered CEO. He stepped up to unveil the cars. Not before a speech though. We prepared ourselves. There were buckets of manure mixture to pour. The timing had to be right for the greatest impact. The fliers had to be readied too.

He walked up to the podium with a corporate panache that must have made his juniors aspire even more to be like him: a leader of men, an orator, a man who made dreams come true. His immaculate black suit glistened in the white light that warmed him.

He began his address crisply: 'Thank you all for being here today. You have made this launch a grand success and we hope that in the near future, the XS three oh oh oh, will make headlines as India's top selling luxury car.

'To me there is no greater mark of success than the car you drive. Our models have always been special. Millions of people the world over aspire to own one of our beautiful creations. Millions of people spend their entire lives dreaming of the SHB brand.

'Finally, after a great wait, we have brought our latest line to India!'

'So where is this guy's halo?' Abhay sneered.

'Oh, it only shows in press release photographs and on magazine covers.'

'I see. Is it time yet?'

'Not quite, he's setting it up for us.'

'He's quite full of himself.'

We watched him as he continued.

'I believe the day is not far when every young person in India has this as his dream car. The fine engineering, the slender curves, never before has a machine been so blatantly desirable.'

That was the cue for some major activity backstage. The organizers scrambled to get the second level of the stage moving. It was time for the cars to be brought under the light and for the white satin sheets that draped them to be pulled off.

Robin Kapoor raised his right hand to the sky.

'This is your time. This is your moment. Seize it. You too can be the proud owner of the world's greatest automobile ever. I give you, the XS three oh oh . . .'

He didn't know what hit him. Before he could reach 'oh' number three, Robin Kapoor, the great businessman, stood covered in dung, his raised right hand dripping with the stench of a thousand cows' refuse, his face smeared in chocolate paste. He stood motionless, dumbstruck.

Then it was the turn of the cars. One by one we emptied the buckets over the stage.

Falling straight through, twenty storeys down, it crashed through windscreens, light panels and speakers. In the midst of it all we threw down our pamphlets and fliers. They fluttered about in the sky above the hysterical mass of people running amok below us.

People ran in every direction, screaming and crying.

'What the fuck is going on?' the once calm Mr Kapoor was now shouting himself hoarse.

The bright blue evening made a wonderful background for the papers coming down on our audience. We had just hijacked the show. It would have been criminal for us to waste the opportunity and not give any indication of why we were doing it all.

'No one needs this shit', 'Sell it like it is', and 'You are not your car' our 'subtle' pamphlets read.

The advertisements had begun. We even signed off with 'Love, Your Anarchists'. Abhay thought it would be a nice touch to have no names, just a simple insignia.

We could hear wails of the assaulted rising up from the stage. They screamed in agony and cried for help. The supermodels in lacy red bikinis stumbled to find the ground again.

People were reading the pamphlets too. The indefatigable media folk had snapped away as the shit rained down. What would have been a fantastic car launch ended with the famed sleek exterior and plush leather interiors getting smeared with copious quantities of fermenting dung. The flashes made a beam of their own; and the headlines were sure to be ours now.

'We've got anarchists in this town. What would have been another evening promoting the new model of the SHB Auto Company has broken out in utter mayhem. Unidentified men dropped large quantities of manure and dung on the stage where the event was taking place, right behind me, right here at the Pirelli Towers in Mumbai not more than ten minutes ago. This event was to mark the launch of SHB's new exquisite line of XS3000s in India.'

'The assailants also dropped fliers and pamphlets like this one.' She held up the 'No one needs this shit' example.

'Is this middle-class India's cry against materialism? Or is this just the work of some kids trying to have fun? Only time will tell. A full-scale investigation has already been unofficially ordered, to try and catch the so-called Anarchists of Mumbai. This is Dhwani Sinha reporting live for NDTV 24x7.'

We had made the most of the chaos that reigned the first few minutes after the dung had hit to make good our escape. We ran down the side of the building, using the fire escape. The race to the back alley was quick. There wasn't any time to stop and think. We had just a few minutes before the building security swarmed all over searching for the 'troublemakers'. We reached the bus stop behind us and boarded the next big red that came our way. We were lucky.

I felt like a deaf, blind and mute man running in circles, alone on a deserted island, beating his only metal pot with a candle for attention. Waves lapped at my dirty ankles. The sea breeze whipped across my weather-beaten torso as the tireless sun burnt my nose mercilessly. I smiled. It dawned upon me that there was no one coming for me. There was no bottle oscillating its way to the shore and there were no ships vacillating in the distance. It was just me. I put down the candle and threw away the pot. I walked determinedly in what I hoped was the direction of the ocean. I chose the tide. I chose not to lie on the beach and complain. I dived right in. Not a hope, not a whimper, not a prayer.

The banana-plastering exercise had begun.

12. THERE IS SUCH A THING AS GOOD TELEVISION

It was a modest tea stall. Kishan Pandey, the shop's nosey owner, was known to dryly inform people that his shop served the best garma-garam chai in the locality and the most delicious bun–anda in the city. No one contradicted him. The tea was sweet and seared your throat as you drank it and the buns were soft and buttery.

He stood behind his table and boiled eggs in a deep pan alongside the large kettle perennially on the boil. The bright turquoise walls complemented the grey and brown benches. In an age of fancy Baristas and Café Coffee Days, this was where the everyman sat and enjoyed his beverage in the company of friends.

A pensive policeman sat at the head of a table of raucous locals on a tea break. Their animated discussion was interspersed with enormous bouts of laughter.

'I don't know if it was horse manure or cow dung,' the cop clarified for his audience.

'But it sure stank all the way from there to here. Can you still smell it?' The local wit snickered.

'I can.' The policeman was firm.

'Yes, yes, Akram bhai has a fantastic sense of smell, after all he's a policeman . . .'

'Are you making fun of me?' barked Akram. He was clearly not having a great day. Just that morning his boss had called him about the case. At 6 a.m.

'We're looking for those punks,' he continued seriously, swirling the chai around in his glass as he talked. 'Apparently their little drama has upset some of the higher-ups in the government as well as in my department. There's a full-scale top-level investigation that has been launched. Those SHB guys are too well connected to not have something done immediately.'

His eyes flamed as he looked over his friend's shoulder to see the tiny television behind him, bringing them a trailer of the latest Johnny C film.

'What does that mean? "Full scale, top level." Every bloody enquiry is immediate, full scale and top level. How many of these enquiries really work, Akram bhai?' The stall owner mocked him. He had clearly been following the conversation. 'I don't understand how they could have made their way around all that security.'

'Don't tell anyone, but we found two janitor's uniforms abandoned on the stairs at the back,' Akram added in a hushed voice, conspiratorially leaning in towards the avid audience.

'The ones that open up into Main Street?' the hearty gentleman to his left spoke loudly.

'Yes, the long spiral staircase at the back,' the inspector said, visibly surprised.

'I read about that in the paper!'

'What?'

'Yes, it seems your confidential bit of "inside information" is doing the rounds. It's been all over the papers for the past week!'

The policeman looked down into his glass of tea in embarrassment, shrugging his shoulders. His satanic goatee aided him in his characteristic scowl. Sensing his displeasure his friends began goading him more.

'You have to admire their courage, Akram bhai . . .' they started only to be interrupted by a loud outburst from the beleaguered cop.

'You people are out of your minds, giving these boys, these vandals, a pedestal to dance on and celebrate their pranks.'

'Oh let it go, he's just yanking your chain.' Pandey advised as he bustled about behind the counter pouring piping hot tea into glasses.

'I will let it go if he does. Everyone has their two bits to throw in, how the police should work, how the government should function . . .' Akram sullenly muttered.

'Don't we elect the honourable men in white that your department runs around night and day to protect and serve?' Pandey shot back.

'You sure do . . . you're in control . . . yes, yes . . . nothing would happen without our Mr Pandey here . . .'

'Shhh . . .'

'Let me speak, this man ought to be put in his place.'

'You have to see this.' It was Arjun, the little helper boy at the chai stall. He was pleading with everyone around him to pipe down and look at the television.

There was something different playing.

Everyone's attention was drawn to the little screen up in the corner.

'What? What happened?' they asked him.

'Look at the TV!' he insisted.

Akram was the first to realize what was going on.

On the screen there was a chair in front of a plain white wall. On the wall was a banner. The banner read 'The Anarchist Project', in bright red on a black background. A traditional Rajasthani puppet, the kind you see on the road almost every other day lay motionless on the chair.

'Turn it up! Turn it up!' they shouted to Arjun as he scrambled to place a chair in front of the television, in order to reach for the volume button. He succeeded, nearly tipping over and falling in his excitement.

This is you, my friend. This is what you look like . . .

A loud booming voice took over the airwaves, the recording quality was not fantastic, and there was a minor hiss in the background.

We hate to interrupt this broadcast. We're sure the dancing and singing will resume soon after we're taken off air.

We must get this communiqué through in time.

I represent the Anarchist Project. You may have heard of us in the news recently . . .

The puppet rose and stood in the chair. He raised his hand and the camera zoomed in on him.

For long the iniquities of the government and the media have played their tricks on us. For far too long have we been subjected to the strategic subjugation campaign carried out by the powers that be.

'I can't believe it. Those bastards are on bloody television!' exclaimed Akram as the screen showed a white gloved hand controlling the puppet as it started its dance.

We've been programmed to think in certain ways by sources that aren't even fully aware of their potential and are usually being used without them knowing it.

'Shhh . . .'

Akram stepped out of the tea shop and stared at the busy road. He saw some bewildered people huddled around the television sets in the shop across the road.

'We've got to put an end to this. Arjun beta, what channel is it?'

'Now 95, sir.'

'Thanks. Now keep watching it. The show's about to change.'

Steel in his veins he began a determined walk towards his bike, pulling out his walkie-talkie and requesting backup. He wanted the entire Mumbai Police to descend upon Now 95's offices all over the city.

His burgeoning belly wobbled in his haste. The vibrations of his motorcycle didn't help.

'Must start exercising more regularly . . .'

His friends from the chai stall watched him with interest as he sped off.

'Good luck, Akram bhai!' some shouted.

'He won't catch them. They'll be long gone.' Pandey sniggered.

'But the broadcast is still on, maybe he'll make it in time.'

'I hope he doesn't!' a tiny voice from the back sparked up. It was Arjun, smiling sheepishly with a glint in his eyes.

The broadcast boomed louder, a neighbouring mechanic had opened his garage and put the channel on his loudspeaker.

The one thing that has forever held man to ransom by means of his own pathetic desires is greed. The one intrinsic flaw that has driven him to folly since time immemorial is his own restlessness.

Fake monopoly money fluttered down on the puppet as he moved from side to side, trying to catch the notes. Unsuccessful, he sat down on the chair, tired and defeated. He started to hit his head with his wooden hands. The loud knocks made by the hands connecting with the head were picked up by the microphones and could be heard.

Today the media, your government, your friends and your family are all helpless, hapless tools of a system that stokes wants and ignites a passion for this restlessness. Recognition, respect and even retribution come in units of things and items that we can possess. We've got magazines, advertisements, billboards and movies telling us what we want. We're told what to desire and we're repeatedly told where to get it.

It is time, my fellow citizens of this market of a nation, to hear a counter opinion. It is time to balance the streams of bullshit that are fed to us every hour of every day.

We don't need them. We don't need their system. We don't need entire lives to be based on the pursuit of that car. It is ridiculous that a means for transportation is such a status symbol. It is sad that things embody our aspirations. It is unfortunate that we believe things alone will make us happy. What we do for these things is even worse.

Sirens accompanied the broadcast as a sea of khaki-clad warriors marched into the channel's office. All the exits were blocked off; armed policemen with their weapons at the ready stationed themselves at every conceivable exit. Other television channels' crews arrived and general disorder swept across the busy streets, bringing traffic to a standstill.

Akram had parked his bike at the rear entrance. He panted up the stairs, expecting a gunfight with the evil dung-slingers.

It is to counter the relentless restlessness manufacturers that I, with my compatriots, led an assault on the recent SHB car launch at the Pirelli Towers on the 23rd of June.

There will be more such actions, to show our brothers and sisters that greed must be defeated. There is more to live for. We will systematically attack and paralyse the system; we will choke it with its own fodder. We will feed it till it bursts.

The camera now zoomed in towards the banner. The words 'The Anarchist Project' were spread across the screen.

We would like to clarify that we are not affiliated to any party. We don't belong to any organization.

We are you. We are your angst. We are your Anarchists. We will be heard.

Akram led his men in, checking every room as they inched closer and closer to the row of programming rooms inside the channel's broadcast headquarters.

They were met with the sight of a middle-aged man. His shirt was half tucked into his pants, and he seemed exhausted.

'It's locked, sir, there's no way to enter the room. We tried breaking it down and entering but didn't succeed. They might be armed.'

'Which room, where are they?'

'PCR 2, it is down this way,' he pointed back.

'Take us there. Why haven't you cut the broadcast? Cut the power . . . cut the damn power.'

'We can't, sir, that would disrupt all the other channels that we are supporting.'

'Who cares?'

'My bosses don't want to be sued for paid airtime by every advertiser.'

He was helpless. He looked like he had tried everything.

Akram and his men doubled their speed, thanks to the flustered employee. He was quite worried.

'I hope she's okay.'

'Who?'

'Shahnaz, it was her shift that they hijacked. It was a chunked show of film trailers. Everyone else is at Ms Shankaran's recording in PCR 1.'

'Ms Radha Shankaran?' They walked briskly down the corridor as he led them.

'Yes, Radha Shankaran is in the building, she's still singing in there. I saw it all . . . I was in PCR 2 with Shahnaz the whole time. I just walked out to take a leak and when I came back, they were on air and the door was locked,' he concluded piteously. The hand-wringing was the ultimate touch.

'I'm going to lose my job over this . . . we're all going to get fired . . .'

'We'll take care of it. Advani, please take this gentleman to safety. Sir, calm down.'

The communiqué had ended a few minutes ago. The silence in the long corridor was interrupted only by the trotting sound of hard boots hitting the ground. The trotting ceased. The stillness of the programming room was deathly.

'Come out with your hands in the air,' shouted Akram.

'We promise not to hurt you, you are under arrest!'

There was no answer.

'Come out, you coward! Bloody prankster . . . two-bit crook out to save the world!' Akram was giving it his all.

'Sir, I think it's a soundproof room . . .' suggested Mukherjee, Akram's trusted junior.

'Shut up!'

'We're coming in.'

With that they began breaking the door down. Large pieces of furniture had been placed in front of it, blocking entry to the room even after the door had been broken in.

'What the hell is going on? Remove it all.'

Mukherjee and the other policemen went to work. They struggled with the door, the couch, and the table and finally made their way into the main soundproof chamber.

There lay Shahnaz sprawled over the Vision Mixer, her head down on it.

'They aren't here, the bastards got away!'

'Check on the girl, is she okay?'

'She's breathing, looks like she was drugged, sir!'

'Bastards!'

The dejected policeman scanned the room only to realize that the emergency fire escape window had been smashed open. Shards of dark glass lay strewn about on the floor and through the window you could see the landing for the fire escape ladder.

'We're too late.'

13. THE FIRE PRIOR

'You do realize that this is dangerous?' I said.

'I do,' she snapped.

'Are you sure you want to be in on it? We could break in and do the needful.'

'That would be even more dangerous, Pranav, and unnecessary too. Do you want my help or not?'

'Of course, I do.'

'Then it has to be done this way.'

She was a brilliant accomplice, my dear old friend and by far the bravest woman I knew. It was Shahnaz to the rescue, all the way. She had it all worked out; a well-timed alteration in the close circuit television system, some insane toiling with furniture followed by an act of self-intoxication that most WWF wrestlers would shy away from.

'You don't have to do anything, just pass me the minitape and adapter well in time.'

'And the liquid.' Abhay was fidgeting about.

'Yes that too, make sure the bottle doesn't leak in my bag, there will be traces otherwise. I may also faint on my way there.'

'Listen to Agatha here!' I turned to Abhay as he smiled.

I wrote and rewrote the piece for the communiqué. Somewhere along the way it became *our* communiqué. I liked that there were people willing to go the distance with me.

'Do you want to burn the puppet in the video and film it at the end?' she joked.

'For what? We're trying to free him, not kill him,' I sneered.

'For drama, Pranav, drama!'

Asking her for help in the beginning was not easy. First she laughed at the thought that we were the Anarchists.

'You guys?'

'I would never have thought, Mr Expensive Ad-exec and Captain Chemical would do anything but sell Swarovski or pollute God's green earth.'

'I swore off the Swarovski pretty early in life . . . was just looking for some purpose and realized I had it with me ever since I was a teen. Captain Chemical here is coming in handy as he is.'

'Hmm, I never thought he'd be able to do what he wanted . . . Anyway you both used to talk a lot about mad schemes like this!' Abhay justified.

'Good to see you're getting into it now,' she snickered.

'He still talks a lot,' Abhay observed, with a solemn look in his eyes.

'I bet he does, our man invented his own language when we were what . . . eight?'

She had been my friend since the time we used to climb trees and play in parks. We had our own special language, even a form of karate that was unknown to the rest of the world; until we realized how lame we were.

She read the announcement to herself.

'Tone it down a bit.'

'Why?' I asked.

'Not the message, the language. You want to be understood by everyone, right?'

'Yes.'

There was a very wide range of people that tuned into her channel. Their TRPs were through the roof. The slot was ideal for hooking up with a massive audience.

We just needed to be careful and to squeeze in our material at the right moment. At first I was unsure if she could manage that. I was also a bit worried about getting her involved in general, but all my doubts were put to rest by her disarming confidence and intrepid determination.

'You don't understand,' she assured us. 'This is what I would like to say on air myself!'

'I had no idea . . .' I smiled knowingly.

'Yeah, I would probably get fired the same day. We're practically going to get away with murder here, if all goes well.'

'Well, that's an inane thing to say. What could possibly go wrong?' said Abhay smugly.

Fortunately, it didn't.

14. JAMES BROWN KNOWS THAT
I FEEL GOOD

'I didn't know what was happening, he just came up from behind me and before I knew it there was a hanky in my face. I can still smell the terrible fumes . . . my back up had just gone to the bathroom . . .' Shahnaz gripped her throat and coughed, her agony was real. Seated on a hospital bed, she answered the policeman's queries as best she could.

'It was chloroform, crude, possibly home-made. Did you get a look at him, his hands, his clothes, anything?' Akram growled.

'No, no I didn't. He wore gloves though, they were white surgeon's gloves.'

'Yes, we found them in the dustbin next to you.'

'They must have been waiting outside for an opportune moment, to get in and play their video,' she pondered aloud.

'Did anyone catch a glimpse of them? As they escaped or entered . . . anything?' Her honest eyes were moistening. Her basic theatrical prowess came in handy.

'No. Strangely no one saw anyone suspicious come through. We're looking into it. Even the close circuit televisions are not showing any unidentified people. It's really baffling.'

'Crooks,' she pronounced, gravely.

'They broke the large window in the waiting area in your office.'

'Oh, they must've gone out through it . . .'

'Right.' The policeman stared down at the green linoleum floor, lost in thought.

'Did they say anything to you?' he asked hopefully.

'No . . . at least I don't remember anything.'

'Lastly, ma'am, do you know of anyone who might be capable of this?'

'What do you mean?'

'I mean, is there someone you suspect? We're just trying to figure out why they chose your channel . . . and your show.'

'We have a lot of viewers . . . Mr?' she said, proudly.

'Akram.'

'Mr Akram. I don't know anyone capable of doing this stuff.'

'Thank you. We hope you feel better soon.'

'Thank you. I hope you catch them.'

They left despondently. Shahnaz smiled to herself.

'What a dump. I hate hospitals!' she stared up at the tube lights above her bed.

'But a girl can change . . .' muttering the American sitcom cliché to herself, she curled up in her blanket.

A nurse entered the room and asked, 'How are you now, Shahnaz?'

She just slept calmly. In her head James Brown was singing about how good he felt.

ψ

I too lay resting in my apartment. The view from my bedroom had never looked better. I nodded off and fell into a deep dream. It was a sincere dream. I wafted through the air on a busy road, watching people around me. Everyone shouted out to me.

'I hear you!' they cheered.

They pulled a cart behind them. There was an enormous, beautiful white horse on top of it. This was no Trojan. It was a real horse. It's gorgeous mane waved in the sunlight as the gentle wind lifted it and made it bounce. The people in front of the cart toiled on. The beast on board neighed and blew out from its cavernous nostrils. On either side of the path were long stretches of undulating green meadows.

'We hear you!' they shouted.

One by one, they started stepping back from the cart. With a look of relief on their faces they moved to the side of the path. The horse on the cart stood unmoving.

It was a beautiful requiem in anticipation of the changes we all wanted. I smiled in my sleep, as I felt my self-esteem return.

15. GREEN IS THE COLOUR OF LOVE

'Do you mind carrying one of these bags? I'm carrying all of them and they weigh a ton,' Abhay whined.

'Hold on, I'm trying to figure out the best route to take.' I was pondering over a map.

'My hands are hurting.'

'Let's stop for a bit then, put the bags down.'

'Didn't he draw you a map with his favourite places?' The scorn in his voice was evident.

'As far as he's concerned, there is no official record of these places.'

'I suppose they don't have a filing system for sources of bribes.'

'They should! Since it's such a widely accepted "we don't know you exist, you don't come out of this place" policy.'

We stopped below one of the lamp posts that lit up the roadside with their pale orange light.

'Now that's the way to Mariana Street.' I gestured towards my right.

'Looks like a fucking dungeon.'

'Probably is one.'

'How exactly are we going to find these guys?'

'The pimps?'

'Yeah ... I'm not sure they'll want to talk to us.'

'Please, they're all "businessmen", right? We'll just talk business with them.'

'Just like your piece?' Abhay was getting aggravated again.

'Yes.'

'You think that will work?'

'I know it will.'

We marched up Mariana Street. The dark alley was straight out of hell. The stench from the gutters was unbearable. The curtains in front of windows were still and calm. So many windows, so many lights inside. Women peered down at us as we walked up to a rickety ochre door. Apparently, the owners of the establishment had a sense of humour. Scribbled on the door was 'No one can come just once'.

A scary-looking bouncer of sorts guarded the door. His bald pate made a silhouette against the dark background of the red baroque wall behind him. We could see his belly from afar too.

'What do you want?'

'We'd like to see the boss,' I said as confidently as I could manage.

'And I'd like to fuck Mallika Sherawat. Get the fuck out of here.'

'Listen, you don't understand, we're all about profit here. We have a business proposition.' It was a sea change from the fumbling Abhay I knew. He was deep into his sales pitch as the bewildered bouncer listened.

'This is my friend Ajeet, I myself am Shakaal. If we could just meet your boss, life would be a lot easier for all of us.'

It was good to see him on a roll. Fortunately, he didn't name one of us Mogambo.

'What business proposition?'

'We'd rather speak to someone in charge. There is good money to be made here.'

'Okay, wait here.'

He turned to open the door but stopped halfway.

'If you two are cops, there will be hell to pay because we already have a nice arrangement with some nice people in your department.'

We kicked into our fake laughs and denied the accusations.

'I hate cops!'

'Cops should die.'

Abhay went a bit overboard with that.

The giant guard didn't look pleased.

'Wait here,' he snarled.

We hung around outside for about five minutes.

'Wish you'd be cool about this, Abhay.'

'Sorry, it isn't every day that I get to go to a friggin' brothel and meet the other side of life.'

'Right, now before we get made and get carried out of here wrapped in white satin, just try to relax.'

'Get made? Who are you? Donnie Brasco?'

'Quiet, I think I can hear someone coming.'

There was a loud clang in the distance, behind the door. We could hear footsteps getting louder, someone seemed to be climbing down stairs.

I guess one of the added benefits of being a raging Anarchist is the guaranteed adrenaline rush. We wanted to make this little endeavour extremely special. We wanted it to go perfectly. Abhay's characteristic left leg twitch of excitement was back. He had really been a quivering pillar of support. A true friend. A new man.

'Relax, da!' I told him.

'Dei! What are you ... trying to relate to me?'

'For the millionth time, is it "da" or "dei"?'

'It fucking varies.'

A booming voice from the inside interrupted our nervous banter.

'Who the heck wants me?'

Then there was silence for a bit.

Abhay started fidgeting.

'This is the first time I'm meeting a pimp.'

'Shut up, Shaakal. Follow my lead.'

The silence was eerie now.

'What is up with those names?' I began again.

'Nothing. I just panicked. Can't tell him our real names now, can we?'

'No, no, you did good ...'

The door opened with a loud burst, and under the archway stood a short man, his most glaring feature being his enormous eyes. They peered at us, whiter than most clouds, larger than most eggs. The bouncer stood behind the little man, his arms crossed.

'I said, who wants me?' It was hard to imagine such a deep baritone from such a puny-looking man.

'Sorry sir, hope we aren't interrupting anything.'

'You land up unknown and unannounced, obviously you're going to be interrupting something. What the fuck do you want?'

'Relax sir, we're just here to ask you for help. We have a proposition for you.'

'Usually, I am the one who makes the propositions.'

'Well sir, Mr . . .'

'You don't need my name. Get to the point.'

'Mr . . . Mr Pimp sir, we were wondering if you would let us use your brothel as an outlet for our merchandise.'

'What? What merchandise? Stop wasting my fucking time. Murli!' he called out to his bouncer.

'We have a lot of things, we have a condom dealership and some very interesting new products for your clients. Right from toys to paans,' I interjected.

'Paans?'

'Yes sir, it's an extraordinary paan that invigorates and energizes,' Abhay piped up.

'It would be ideal for the tired and weary souls that venture here, seeking entertainment, looking for some time off from their lives . . .' I started the story.

'Their jobs . . .' Abhay chimed in.

'Wives . . . kids . . . bills.'

'I get the picture!' the evil little man piped up.

'What else have you got?' He tried to look unimpressed.

'We have a pretty good network.'

'Network?' he scoffed. 'You'll be surprised at my present clientele.'

'We know you already have a great presence in the market, sir.'

'Who told you that?'

'No one, no one who means any harm, sir.'

'Go on, what can you do for me? What's your name?'

'I'm Ajeet. Like I said, we can get you great bulk jobs. What I mean is that I have a close friend who works at one of the top hotels here. He has to make arrangements quite often for his guests. I was wondering if we could work out a deal. I'll manage the orders and transportation, all you have to do is supply the girls.'

'That sounds interesting.' He stared at me, looking me up and down. 'You don't seem like a man in this business.'

'Neither do you, sir.'

'Hmmm . . . It would be good to have a system in place to transport the girls without getting caught . . . How many orders are we looking at?'

'Oh, don't worry about that, sir, we'll work out the exact details later. So you're okay with our proposal?'

'Tell me more about the products you want to sell.'

'Oh, they're state-of-the-art sex toys, shipped in from Japan,' Abhay said as he whipped out a purple dildo.

The pimp laughed a bit, pushing it back into Abhay's bag.

'Hmm . . . and what about the paans? Why do I need a paan store inside my building, there are so many on the street.'

'That's where you're mistaken, sir. The paans are our creation. They're special paans that are designed to increase the pleasure of your clients. If you want details, I can pass you a brochure. Shaakal, get it out, will you . . .'

Abhay reached into one of the bags and pulled out our beautiful eight-page brochure on the wonders of our paans. God bless InDesign. He held it out for the greasy man who stood before us. Flipping through the brochure, the pimp instructed his bald bouncer to fetch his reading glasses for him.

'Well, I must say that I am impressed by your professionalism!'

'Oh we're just passionate about what we sell. All the inspiration comes from there.'

'I see. Well I would invite you boys in, but there's no place to just sit and talk right now. I'm thinking of getting that place there too . . .' He pointed to another building down the road. 'It's a bit run-down, but I think I can bring it back to life, if you know what I mean.'

We looked at each other. There was a phrase on loop in my head: to reform a system you must become a part of it. To reform a system you must become a part of it.

Hello, grindstone.

The thick pimp glasses brought from his pimp chambers perched on his nose as he read through the brochure.

'This could definitely boost my business more.'

'That's right! It would also give you that competitive advantage, by improving the quality and diversity of the service you provide,' I chirped helpfully.

'What?'

'It's good for you and your clients.'

'Right!'

'So do we have a deal?' We already knew the answer.

'Yes, I think we do. Come back tomorrow morning and we'll talk more about money, arrangements and how to go about our business. Partners!'

'Great, here's a little something to get you started and to let you know how serious we are about working with you. It's a bag of our paans. They're fresh and they'll keep you fresh too.'

'Hey! That could be a good tag line.'

'Hmm . . . Waah! I think I'll try one myself,' he said as he stepped forward and peered into the bag with a huge smile on his face.

He picked up a paan and put it in his mouth. His style was natural and from it one could see that he enjoyed a good paan. He smacked his dirty red lips and shook his head in appreciation from left to right.

'Murli! Have one, it is mind-blowing!'

'Thank you, sir!' The big bouncer stepped forward and daintily popped a paan into his mouth. 'This is good.'

'Yes, I suggest you hand them out to all your clients today. It'll be good to get them hooked,' Abhay added, slyly.

'I like that idea. Murli, I want you to give one of these to every man who comes through here tonight. If they refuse tell them it's invigorating. Say it's a gift from me. Okay?'

'Yes boss.'

'And give these nice gentlemen, Mr Ajeet and his friend here, my mobile numbers.'

He then turned to us and said that we could call him any time.

'How much for tonight's paans?'

'They're complementary, sir.'

'Nonsense, tell me how much they are for. I will pay you.'

A pimp who was keen to pay; never thought we'd meet one like him. Then he stepped closer to us and whispered.

'Promise me you won't go to anyone else with this proposal.'

'We wouldn't think of it.'

'Good. Now how much do I owe you?'

'It's about Rs 7 a piece, there are about two hundred in there.'

'I'll give you a thousand five. Murli, get the money.'

Murli returned shortly with the promised dough.

'You want something else for the night?' he winked at us.

'No thank you, sir, we have an early day tomorrow.'

'Besides we never mix business with pleasure.'

'Then you are in the wrong place, because my business is pleasure itself.' He laughed out loud looking to his goon for validation. He too guffawed in a fit of false joy.

'Okay, I'll see you boys tomorrow morning, it's a pleasure doing business with you . . .' He continued his cackling laughter as we readied to leave.

'Sure, sir.'

We walked away, out of the alley, towards the main road. Our old decrepit van was parked nearby. In it were more paans. More brochures and some interesting sex toys.

Shaakal and Ajeet then went on to make eight more visits that night.

It is remarkable how we always blame the establishments and never hold the patrons responsible for the wrongs that they do. It is perhaps difficult to track them. They don't have a central place or haunt, other than the brothels themselves.

We thus decided to target the assholes that fed the system for a change.

'That makes nine,' I said as we concluded our last meeting of the night and reached our van.

'Yup. Things are looking up,' Abhay concurred as we got in and pulled the doors shut.

We had mailed a little advertisement to all the papers that day, in time to make the next morning's edition. We even made calls to ensure that our 'friends' in the media would in fact print the stuff. Apart from one of them, everyone said yes.

'Things are well in motion now,' Abhay said contentedly as I reversed the van out of the alley.

We could hardly wait to see their faces when it all came together.

16. THE AFTERGLOW

Praveen Deshmukh was a respectable man. He led a good life, with a nice house, two kids and a wife. But Mr Deshmukh was not satisfied with his existence. He always had a keen eye for a bargain and perhaps that is what made his jewellery store so successful.

He woke up at his usual time, around eleven in the morning, and ambled out of his king-sized bed, scratching his privates and tugging at his wedged underwear.

He walked into his marbled toilet and stared into the sink.

Another great day, he thought, on the heels of a great night.

He splashed his face with some water and then looked up at the mirror. He shouted in disbelief. His face was green.

He tried really hard to wash it off, alas; it wasn't on the surface, for the sin was skin deep.

'What the . . . What the hell is this? Shakuntala! Shakuntala! Help! Where are you?'

The wife ran to the rescue, she had a fruit knife and an apple in her hands.

'What? What happened?'

She saw his back, he was bent over the sink.

'My face is green.'

'What?'

He shrieked again. 'My face is green.' His arm muscles clenched in desperation.

'I can't get it off. What the fuck is this? Did you paint me in my sleep?'

'Bastard!' It was her turn to scream.

She walked straight up to him and looked him in the eye.

'Where were you last night?' A cold anger dwelt in her words.

'Not the same shit again, Shakuntala!' he exclaimed. 'I have a serious problem here! I'm meeting some foreign customers today! What am I going to do . . .?'

'Where were you last night?' The anger was giving way to tears and an anguish that began to worry the respectable Mr Deshmukh.

'What is the matter with you? I was at Ashok's. Remember we play cards every Friday night?'

'You were not at Ashok's place,' she cried. 'You were not at Ashok's place!' Her voice was gaining decibels as her anger frothed up. 'Filthy scum. Filthy low-life bastard scum tyrant!'

'Watch your mouth,' he yelled back, bewildered at his meek wife's unusual outburst.

'Wait here, you bastard,' Shakuntala ordered him as she ran out of the bathroom to retrieve the morning's newspaper.

Praveen looked at his face worriedly in the mirror. She returned and threw the paper at him.

'What am I supposed to do with this?'

'Page one, read it.'

The apple was not there in her hands any more; she had come back with only the newspaper and the fruit knife.

'Son of a bitch!' muttered Mr Deshmukh as he read. 'I don't believe it.'

'Fuck you!' she shouted. 'I'll see you in court.'

'Children, children, come here and see what your father has done,' Shakuntala called as she stalked off to pack her suitcase and leave.

'Shakuntala! No!'

The bottom half of page one was a glorious advertisement for everyone to see. There was a picture of a smiley. It was green in colour. Below it was a message:

Green Is the Colour of Love
Any kind gentleman walking around with a green face today is in such a condition because he visited one of the brothels near Mariana Street on the night of the 12th.

Good luck, our green-faced freaks. Deal with who you are and what you have done.

The world's oldest profession continues to flourish because of bastards like you.

Everyone is in on it. Everyone takes a cut.

We just decided to make it all public.

We encourage you to stay home or face the consequences.

One should not have to sell his or her body and soul for a living.

No one will, if no one's buying.

Love,
Your Anarchists

⚘

It had panned out better than we had planned. Hospitals were reporting numerous cases of patients with a 'green rash' walking in for treatment. At the final tally there were about eight hundred cases reported. The media went ahead with weeks of stories about the incident and we were once again in the limelight.

Dhwani Sinha had become NDTV's favourite correspondent for covering our stories. She was considered a bit of an expert on the matter. A few foreign channels had approached her for a commentary on the 'creative protests everyone was talking about in India'.

'I think she likes me,' Abhay said as we watched a special report on the 'Brothel Incident'.

'She doesn't know you, Abhay,' I pointed out sagely.

'She knows a lot about what I do, man.'

'Maybe you should give her a call.'

'No way . . . now shut up, her show is still on.'

'These effects seem to have been caused by consuming a strong dose of the chemical triphenylmethane and certain yet-to-be identified copper compounds. It is a strange new combination that appears to be mildly toxic for humans. I believe it has its roots in the composition of certain commonly used fertilizers that promote the production of chlorophyll in plants. The Anarchists must have modified its concentration as the final chemical administered, though low in toxicity, is really high in its ability to cause coloration. Those who are affected by it must have ingested it. First, it would have coloured their tongues, and then the effects would slowly have spread outwards, to the gums, lips and finally the skin on their faces. At my clinic there were a few patients who turned up with the green coloration spreading downwards even as far as their navels and up their arms. My guess is that they were fed the chemical through paans to prolong the contact of the agents with their tongues, increasing absorption and exposure. The irritation and itching caused can be easily cured. The bad news is that I am not sure if the pigmentation effects will ever completely go.'

'Thank you Dr Bhatia. I'm sure our viewers will find that information useful,' Dhwani said and smiled at the camera.

'She's so beautiful.' It was Abhay again.

'Abhay . . .' I warned him playfully.

Dhwani turned to the camera and started:

'Yes, right here in Mumbai, the Anarchists have struck again. This time their target of choice is the large number of men frequenting illegal or decriminalized brothels in the city's red-light districts. In an attempt to publicly shame and single out these people, we believe the Anarchists fed them a radical new chemical, through harmless-looking paans. The consumption of the chemical resulted in the green coloration we see here in these photos . . .' Dhwani trailed off as some specimen photos flashed on the screen.

The voiceover continued, 'If you are suffering from this condition, our in-house medical consultant advises you to visit a doctor immediately.'

It was smooth sailing from there. The headlines kept pouring in:

'The Anarchists Claim Mumbai'
'Consumerism, Prostitution, Marketing'

'Selling It Right'
'A New Form of Rebellion'
'Who are the Anarchists?'
'Vandalism Sparks Debates'

The *Times of India* had a near regular feature on us. It was asking people what we should take on next. There was a poll and people were writing in. The *Hindustan Times* wrote about different types of protest, public–political statements over the ages.

It was great to see the support that we had garnered through our activities.

There was a debate on. There were questions being asked. There were problems being recognized. Our detractors lambasted us and our supporters defended our actions vehemently. Fruition? Not quite yet.

Shahnaz saw to it that they introduced a call-in segment for a show on Now 95. They put her in charge of it and she spent a lot of her time answering questions about the Anarchists. She was finally in front of the camera, instead of sitting behind it.

In the midst of it all sat Akram.

'First they drop dung on my ministers, then they kidnap the airwaves of one of our most watched television channels and now this . . . triphenyl whatever . . . this is total complete bullshit. What is this nautanki? What the hell do these people think of themselves?' he raged.

'A bunch of miscreants. That's all they are. Vagrants,' he said as he took a huge swig of his extra-hot glass of tea.

He turned to Mukherjee, his trusted junior. 'What do you think? What do you make of all this?'

'I think there are many other criminals out there who have done much worse things.'

'So you do agree with me. These boys are criminals to you too.'

'Not exactly, sir, they haven't harmed anyone as such . . . nothing really life threatening or anything. They are just speaking their minds, making sure people listen to them, pay attention to them.'

'They are cowards who are laughing at us. This is their sadistic little game . . .' Akram bellowed.

'What about guys like Basu and Sarkar?' Mukherjee pointed at the photographs on the notice board in the police station.

'What about them?'

'They are wanted for multiple homicides, sir. I think they're laughing at us louder than the Anarchists,' he argued with Bengali panache.

'It's been several years and we haven't been able to get them,' his boss admitted. 'But those two are a different kind of scum. At least I have their photographs here. I know who I am up against. I know how they work. But these guys . . .' He lifted a newspaper. 'These guys are playing dirty.'

'What is the real problem, sir?' Mukherjee asked astutely, sensing that Akram wasn't revealing everything.

Akram fell back in his chair and looked up at his map of India beside him. 'I have received orders from above.'

The tension gleamed on his forehead. The old, murdered ceiling fan screeched along in the brief moment of silence, degree by degree. 'I have received orders to shoot them at sight.'

'The Anarchists? They've done nothing!'

'Speak softly.' Akram gritted his teeth.

'The number of people that they have managed to annoy is incredible. From corporates, big guys with big money in imported suits, to the vermin of the underworld, they're all out to use my gun and me to get these boys. There are different kinds of pressure being applied, Mukherjee. You have no idea . . .'

The younger man chuckled. 'I see, sir. But what good is a shoot-at-sight order, if you don't know what they look like? Fortunately, none of us can identify them.'

'Fortunately?'

'We can't do it, sir.'

'I have to deliver results soon. Else we'll be castigated. Transferred. Shamed by the mad media of this city and nation.'

'The media loves these boys, sir.' Mukherjee was stating the obvious and he knew it.

'Of course they do. They're getting unusual stories regularly, they've got a cult to build and sell. But the mediawallahs are fickle. Unka koi bharosa nahin. At present they are in the Anarchists' camp, but who knows what will happen later. We only know one thing: for better or for worse, we can't escape them.'

'Let's go talk to the television channel lady again.'

'Shahnaz Khan?'

'Yes. We may have missed something the first time around. It's the only lead we've got to go on.'

17. BUILDING MY 'CAR'MA

Abhay woke up late that day. He came out of his room looking like he had been in a plane crash.

'I have a terrible headache,' he proclaimed in the hoarsest voice I had ever heard.

'No, you don't!' I shot back.

'Ah, Pranav's power of suggestion at its best. Thanks, man, I feel a lot better.'

'What do you want? A hug?'

He poured himself a glass of cold water; he took his first sip, not before requesting me to shut up.

'How are you not reacting to this? Have you gone blind?' I asked, affronted at how easily he seemed to have ignored the scene in the living room.

He looked up at me. His expression of melancholy changed to one of surprise.

'What on earth is going on in here?'

'Essay number three, "Corruption and its rats",' I announced.

Never before had our ordinary drawing room been filled with such a wide array of items. He took a quick pan of everything that lay around me.

'Fuck! Is that a real rat?'

'That's Larry. Moe and Curly are back there.'

'What is the matter with you? Most people try to get rid of rats and you just brought an entire family on board here . . .'

'Calm down, they're all in separate cages.'

'It's far too early in the morning for all this. I need some Jam.'

'I need more buckets. These won't do the trick. By the way, we have got to do this tonight.'

'I can't wait,' said my excited partner in crime while pushing in his 'Vs.' CD.

Before he could press play, the phone rang.

It was Shahnaz and she was not extremely appreciative of his curt and moody 'Hello'.

'Who peed in your rasam Mr Krishnan?'

'Uh, no one . . . and we drink coffee in the morning; the day doesn't begin and end with rasam.'

'My humble apologies,' she effused.

'Talk to her,' he said distractedly as he threw the receiver to me and went on to blast 'Dissident'.

'Hi Shahnaz! How are things this fine morning?'

'I just wanted to tell you guys that Inspector Akram and his little helper man Mukherjee came to my office today.'

'Hmm . . . how come?'

'They waited for my entire show, in the room outside. They've still not fixed the window in there, you know?'

'What did they want to talk to you about?'

'The same old questions.'

'It's probably not safe to talk on the phone then. Where are you?'

'I'm still in my office.'

'Okay,' I said as I thought of how we could meet and talk without raising any flags on Akram's radar.

'I'm done with work till about three now. I'll need to come back by then.'

'That's cool. Abhay will pick you up in about twenty minutes.'

'What? Why?' he shouted from the kitchen.

'I need some stuff for the next . . .'

'The next?' Shahnaz asked excitedly. 'What are you guys doing this time?'

'Quiet.'

'I'll head out as soon as I finish my coffee,' Abhay grumbled.

'That's cool. So Shahnaz, he'll come by in about an hour then. With Abhay, coffee usually includes other ablutions too.'

'You bet,' he reiterated.

'Not a problem. See you soon,' Shahnaz said as she hung up. I put the phone down.

'What could the cops possibly want with her, so many days after the incident?' I thought aloud.

'Maybe they're on to us. Maybe they're waiting outside now!' He was perturbed and more awake now.

I tried to reassure him in my most professional and matter-of-fact manner.

'No one's waiting outside. Here's a list of the things we need. I'm going to firm up the sequence, locations and work out the issues that we currently face with this.'

'Yes sir. Never did a corporal have a better lieutenant, sir.'

'You aren't a corporal, Abhay. You're . . .'

'It's okay, señor. No need to explain. I was just kidding. Now if you'll excuse me, I must relieve myself.'

He left the room.

The next song on the album was 'Rats'. I smiled to myself and went back to my little clipboard, sketching routes and covering angles. The previous day's recon had proved to be useful.

I had never been fond of ostentatious displays of wealth and well-being. Be it at weddings, in garages or on mantles. It was often the easiest way for the corrupt to invest their ill-gotten gains. Such had been the case with a duo of powerful gentlemen.

Abhay's first job out of university was at a big manufacturing plant called the Royal Bharat Chemical Company. For the first few months he worked and served them diligently. He was one of their rising stars. Time went by and his morale started to wane.

It was at the dosa place that he sat with me and Shahnaz, cribbing.

'It's just not right.'

'Are you sure?'

'I'm absolutely sure.'

'How can they not care?'

'Yeah man, aren't there forms and papers to fill for any refuse to be disposed of?' I asked.

'There are. You have to be cleared by the BEIRC, the Board for Emissions and Industrial Regulation Controls. They send inspectors to the plant who are supposed to ensure that the company is fully compliant with all the rules and regulations regarding toxic waste disposal.'

'I don't understand it then . . .'

'The paperwork is all doctored.'

'You've seen the forms?'

'For the thousandth time, yes! I sat with Mr Chopra in the fucking meeting. We were in the smaller boardroom. Our presentation was quite short and perfunctory. The guys from the regulation department just nodded at everything.' Abhay was seething.

'Go on . . .'

'They removed five slides that I had prepared detailing the harmful effects of the material. It was supposed to be a plan talking about how we were going to handle it, you know . . . fix it, clean it and then dump it. We could make fertilizer from it.'

'They took it out?'

'Yes. They went right ahead and said it was harmless. And those bastard BEIRC inspectors who came and watched me working in the labs had no questions. They told me I was doing a great job.'

'Wow!'

'Yeah . . . I can't work there any more, man. I have to quit.'

'Leave then. Join someone else, you were at the top of your class and this experience ought to hold you in good stead.'

'I'm not worried about getting another job. I'm worried about what they're going to do to that poor village.'

Shahnaz had comforted him and said it was best to walk away.

I had sat there in my rage, my rage that could go nowhere. Until now.

18. TOXIC VEHICLE

They gave it its due importance and built it up better than we could have, had we been the news crew. Dhwani Sinha spoke with immense pride. Her voice quivered as she delivered this little piece over the television; we sat watching it with bated breath.

'Traffic has its own set of problems in Mumbai. More often than not people like you and I have a tough time making our way through the chaotic mess every morning to get to offices, schools and wherever it is the day has to take us.

'Today the roads were jammed for a different reason. This morning, traffic at the junction of Sadiq Road and Shivaji Marg came to a standstill because of a most unusual roadblock. It was the Anarchists once again! And this time they seem to have chosen to take on one of Mumbai's top government officials and also the owner of a growing multinational to make their statement . . .'

The camera moved forward, shifting focus from the presenter to soak in the cause of all the mayhem. It was just as we had left it, only now the frame was swarming with mystified policemen, frenzied reporters and a clique of camerapersons cataloguing every inch of the spectacle in their cameras. Dominating the scene were two 'beautiful', enormous cars parked such that they were jamming all three lanes of Shivaji Marg: a gleaming black Mercedes and a shiny silver BMW. Both the cars had a dirty and thick green liquid poured over the back seats. Perched on the roof of the Mercedes was a signboard that had clearly been ripped down from a building; it read 'Royal Bharat Chemical Company'. It was being held in place by a makeshift stand and some rope. The BMW showed a massive blow-up portrait of the same green liquid that was pooling in the interiors of the car pouring out from a grand pipeline, into a pond. The sides of the cars bore our signature, 'the Anarchist Project', in bright red paint. Fumes climbed high from the vehicles and the stench was unbearable. All the onlookers stood cupping their mouths, a policeman in the thick of it was throwing up, his eyes watering.

A brave and determined front for the police department greeted Dhwani and the other reporters clamouring for a sound bite.

'I am sorry. Traffic will have to be diverted through a different route. We can't move the cars yet, our boys are still doing their rounds, gathering evidence and picking up the pieces of this . . . this lurid publicity stunt,' a visibly annoyed Inspector Akram said. 'They've gone too far. From our preliminary enquiries we know that these cars belong to some of the top minds that run this city. This is plain and simple destruction of private property.'

'What is inside the cars, sir?' Dhwani asked.

'Well, you all have to be more patient. We are studying them,' he said and pointed to his deputy, Mukherjee, in the background who was examining the cars. 'As soon as we are able to confirm the nature of the substance, we will inform you.'

Ignoring the circus around him, Mukherjee circled the cars, checking every inch of the road to see if there were any clues. If there had been anything useful, it was long lost, trampled under the feet of the charging army of tamasha-loving onlookers and journalists who had taken over the place before the police had arrived. Shaking his head disappointedly, he then hunkered down and peered into the Mercedes, giving the front seats a thorough once-over. His mask and gloves aided him in examining the mess before him.

'They mutilated it,' he thought to himself as he rummaged through the torn lining of the seats. His hands rested on a box that had been placed near the accelerator, hidden from view. He carefully removed the box from the car and stepped back to gather his thoughts. With silent trepidation he opened the lid and there it was, staring him in the face. A quiet, repugnant and ever so dead rat.

'There's a dead rat in the driver's seat!' he exclaimed.

A laboratory technician who had been deputed to the scene to help gather evidence took a closer look at the box and the dead rat lying in it.

'I think this poor guy probably died overnight, in the car.

There are nibble marks on the inside of the box,' he volunteered helpfully.

'He suffocated?' Mukherjee was confused. 'Stop talking in riddles. What do you mean by he died overnight in the box? There are holes in the box.'

'I could be wrong and we will know for sure only when we test the liquid in the car but I think that the rat choked on the fumes from the liquid. The fumes definitely seem poisonous; we are coughing and gagging standing here. I think the holes lining the top of the box were to let air in. Probably to kill the rat.'

'What a bloody mess! If that liquid is poisonous, we cannot remove any of this without a proper containment unit. And that is going to take forever. I will tell Akram sir to call for the containment people. But first things first, we need to get rid of these fellows,' Mukherjee said as he jerked his head toward the media people crowding around Inspector Akram.

Mukherjee walked over to Guru, a junior deputy in Akram's team, ordering him to get rid of the media. Without batting an eyelid, Guru answered unequivocally, 'No point in asking, Mukherjee sir. Boss is still briefing them and you know as well as I do that these guys won't move till they get all the information.'

But Mukherjee was not paying any attention to Guru. He was looking at the cars and at the sludge on the seats. The pieces of the puzzle were starting to come together in his head. He grabbed Guru who was heading off to herd some photographers away from the cars. 'To hell with them, man. This is starting to make sense to me. I think the gunk on the seats is actual refuse from the plant. Like the photograph up there.'

'Someone is dumping toxic refuse out in the open? In a pond?' Guru's question only drew a miserable look from Mukherjee that confirmed his worst fears. 'Arre sir, this is worse than we thought. We must tell Akram sir immediately.'

'You tell him. This shit could hit a lot of fans.'

'No way, sir. You're his direct junior, you do it.' Guru was in no mood to be in the vicinity of Akram when he heard this news. Akram was known to shoot the messenger.

The content of the reports grew throughout the day. More information kept streaming in and we received a call almost every half an hour from an excited Shahnaz, our only other cohort, to celebrate and laugh about how we'd struck a chord for discord this time. She also warned us about how things were going to get a lot rougher for us.

We didn't care. We were finally doing something that meant more than a monthly paycheck to make bills and buy Gouda with.

'You'd better watch out. They're definitely going to try and get you this time. By hook or by crook.'

'I suppose they already are . . .' Abhay tried comforting himself as he watched the news reports flooding the air waves.

His favourite anchor was back with a full report. Dhwani Sinha was in her element. This time she had viewer responses and a story to tell, a much larger story than the one she started the day with.

'Both cars were stolen last night and the police have been looking for them ever since. They belong to the owner of the Royal Bharat Chemical Company. Mr Amit Chopra and to Mr H.P. Shukla, Chairman of the Board for Emissions and Industrial Regulation Controls.

'At about 6.45 a.m. both the cars were found right at this spot after we and the police received anonymous phone calls declaring their whereabouts. As you can see in the pictures on the screen, the cars had been vandalized. Large quantities of toxic sludge have been poured on the back seat. The police have found a dead rat in a perforated box on the front seat and a package containing photographs showing the dumping of the toxic waste found on the back seat, out in the open, poisoning fields and drinking water sources in villages near Aurangabad and Chiplun.

'Police investigations have confirmed a large quantity of the same sludge being dumped in the outskirts of Mumbai at the Royal Bharat Chemical Company plant. Connections between Mr H.P. Shukla and Mr Amit Chopra are also being investigated further, given that the BEIRC is in charge of ensuring the safe treatment and responsible disposal of all waste materials produced by factories, industrial plants and even workshops. Neither of them was available for comment.

'A search is on to find out the identity of the Anarchists who seem to have dominated the news with their ground-breaking and extreme activities in the recent past.

'We've received numerous emails and SMSs from viewers

all over the world commending the work of the group, praising them for their brave efforts.'

She did an entire feature on the villages too. A few angry farmers spoke about the pipes and the waste that was poisoning their livestock and fields. The expletives flew unabashedly. Just like they should.

'Good job! Great job! These *beeps* should be brought to book, these bloody *beeps* should pay for our cattle and the damage to our fields! At least someone has decided to teach these *beep beep beeps* a lesson. Good for them!'

Amongst all the other specialists, covering issues like wars and political occurrences, the channel now had its own Anarchist specialist.

19. THE KHAKI CONFESSIONAL

The room was reverberating with raised voices. Something heavy was being banged repeatedly on a table to underscore whatever was being said. Whoever was inside, they thought, was getting a sound tongue-lashing and would not come out the same person.

'How can they speak to him like that?' Guru quivered.

'We're in for it now, Guru. We're in for it, for sure,' Mukherjee said with a deep and not entirely unfounded sense of resignation.

'I heard him on the phone this morning, with his bosses; he didn't have much to say then ...' Guru said as he looked at the closed door once again.

'It's the law, what else is new? Big evil monkey clubs smaller monkey and the chain continues from there ...' Mukherjee philosophized.

'Don't you mean big fish eats small fish and so on?'

'Whatever ... I feel like a prize Rohu right now.'

The door banged open and Akram stepped out.

'And here comes the frying pan,' Mukherjee completed.

'Walk,' ordered Akram, striding down the corridor with a look on his face that could have been anger or anguish.

He didn't break his gait to talk to his juniors, they began walking behind him, much like a shoal.

'It is not possible that these hooligans have left us nothing,' he asserted.

His strides were bigger than usual. It was as though he was lunging forth with every step.

Mukherjee and Guru hid their fear and followed him down the corridor.

'Mukherjee, I want a full report on these guys, everything that we have until now, from their modus operandi to the name of the animal whose dung they used, I want everything.'

'Right sir, I have something ready, just compiling the last bits of information from the grand show yesterday.'

'Grand show?' Akram thundered as he skidded to a halt. 'Grand show? Mukherjee, I know the way your mind works. I will not have it.'

They stopped right where they were, huddling in the corridor.

'I can't fathom your appreciation for them,' Akram hissed, trying to keep his voice low, trying to avoid being overheard by the busybody orderlies and other officials milling about in the halls of the Police Headquarters. 'These people are misfits, miscreants out to make our lives hell. Thus far they have had tremendous success in that endeavour of theirs. But I will not have my own officers appreciating and celebrating their exploits.' He underscored that last sentence with forceful jabs in the air in front of Mukherjee's face.

Guru stared at Mukherjee, expecting an outburst, an open war of words where the master and the disciple would have it out once and for all. After all, it was not long ago that he and Mukherjee had discussed the same subject. They both believed in what the Anarchists had done. Not only had they tipped off the police, they had made a statement and captured the airwaves. People were talking about the Anarchists and their exploits. People were asking questions to find out more about all that was wrong.

A fuming Akram and his two juniors blocked off the corridor.

'Do you understand?' Akram barked.

Mukherjee and Guru didn't need an identification manual to recognize a man who had been pushed to the brink. The brave policeman was fast giving way to a trembling, warbling child, begging for support.

'We'll get them, sir. We *will* catch them. Don't worry,' Mukherjee stated, quietly defusing the situation as Guru watched admiringly.

Akram wiped his face with a handkerchief. Then with not the greatest subtlety, went on to wipe the tears from his eyes.

'We have to.' He firmed up and began his lunging stride down the hall and out of the building. 'This is what we have to do. Listen carefully . . .'

They pored over the reports for hours together. After some time they needed a separate table to just keep the empty glasses of tea. They called Dhwani Sinha of NDTV to see if they could get their hands on her tapes from the 'dung incident' and the coverage on the vandalized cars from the day before. The tapes arrived. The three of them sat and viewed them all, over and over again. They lost track of time. They watched the 'puppet show' and furiously prepared notes about all that they saw.

The investigations meandered into many a dead end. For instance Guru thought he had made a breakthrough when he saw the puppeteer's hands trembling.

'He's a smoker! Ha ha! He's a smoker!' He got up from his chair in celebration.

Akram looked at him and deadpanned. 'Yes! We've got him now! Mukherjee go round up all four of Mumbai's smokers while Guru prepares the questions for them.'

Guru sat down, dejected. They ploughed on.

'You know why people like these guys?' a grim Akram blurted out.

'Why sir?' Guru was startled by his question.

'Because they're shaming whoever the common man would like to.'

'True,' Mukherjee added victoriously as his boss continued.

'They are bajaoing smug merchants, patrons of prostitutes, corrupt big shots. Criminals all of them.'

'That's our job, isn't it?' asked Guru.

'It is. And that's why they're wrong, there's a system in place.'

'Why do I get the feeling you're finding it hard to convince yourself about getting these guys?' Mukherjee almost had his hand up to ask for permission for his earnest question.

'Shut up. There's no such thing. I'd be damned if I started sympathizing with those vandals,' insisted Akram.

'Maybe they're like you and me, only they got tired of waiting. Lost faith in the system perhaps,' Mukherjee suggested.

Guru looked at him and then at Akram who had his head in his hands. Sooner or later, one did realize that the 'system' was not entirely conducive to action and progress. Mukherjee and he had accepted that a long time ago, and so had Akram, he suspected. But would he admit it?

'After all that you've seen, sir, haven't you lost faith in the system?' Guru bravely ventured.

'No . . .' Akram pondered aloud. 'No,' he reaffirmed. 'So what if everyone is on the take. So what if people at every level, in every nook and cranny of the system have found a way to mould it and bend it for their benefit. So what?'

'Yeah . . . so what?' Mukherjee and Guru chimed in.

'I know where I stand. I know what I am. That's all that counts. That's all that matters,' Akram said with resolve. The juniors in the room looked at him as he said this. They looked up to him.

'I admire you for that, sir.' Mukherjee was unequivocal. Guru nodded his agreement.

'I won't shoot them. I don't think I can.' Akram crumbled in the face of their admiration.

'Let's hope it doesn't have to come to that, sir,' Mukherjee said.

'Let's hope,' Akram said solemnly. 'Let's all hope.'

20. RETRIBUTION

At the other end of the city, in a darker place, a different kind of deal was being struck, once again, in the name of the Anarchists.

Amit Chopra, the tainted chemical baron, sat in his living room a dejected man. He had been waiting for a call all evening. His whisky glass remained on the table before him, untouched. The dim lighting accentuated his pensive mood. His mobile phone lay beside the glass and he waited for that familiar sound like an expectant father.

It rang like it had never rung before, he thought.

Hurriedly he reached for the contraption and put it to his ear with a flip that would have put Usain Bolt to shame.

The voice at the other end was hoarse.

'Tell me,' it beckoned.

'H-Hello?'

'Yes, tell me . . .'

'Sir, this is Chopra.'

'I called you, I know who you are. What? Is that sludge rotting your brain too?'

'Um . . . I don't have much time to talk. I want you to find

someone for me and I want you to ... to kill them.'
Mr Chopra was nervous.

'Really! Who gave you the idea that I could provide such
a service?'

'Friends of mine.'

'No friend of mine would want me to meet a person like
me.'

'I'm sorry?'

'I'm dangerous. I'll do it. Who is it that you want?'

'I don't know who he or she or they are. I want you to
catch and kill the Anarchists.'

'The what?'

'The Anarchists. The people who did this to me. They're
running wild all over Mumbai. I want you to find them and
make them pay for what they did.'

'You have any idea who your enemies might be?'

'I have a few. But none of them have the ability or guts to
pull something like this off.' Chopra began grinding his
teeth. 'They've cut it all off. No one will work with me any
more,' he snivelled.

'Keep to the point. I don't have the patience for this kind
of whining.'

'My entire export arm is in jeopardy. No one wants to
work with the polluting third world bastard company any
more ...'

'Keep to the point. What am I? Your Duvidha Hotline?'

'I just want you to know that it is extremely important that
whoever brought me here goes to a much worse place.'

'What about the money?'

'Money is not an issue.'

'That's the first nice thing I've heard you say in this entire conversation.'

'Mr Basu, I assure you, if you kill them for me, I will make you a very rich man.'

'Good. Consider it done.'

'Can I call you on this number to check or . . .'

'This is not my number. I don't have a number. No one calls me, I will call you whenever there is need.'

'I understand.'

'Now go cry into your imported whisky.'

'How do you know I'm . . .?'

Basu cut the phone. The annoying monotone was all that greeted Mr Chopra now.

The hit men with a new hit were across the street, peering into Chopra's apartment with a pair of binoculars.

'Let's go, Sarkar.'

'This seems to be quite a promising one, right Basuji?'

'Without a doubt. Look at this fucker's house. He's loaded.'

21. FROM THE STREET UP

They sat around a garish coffee table, digging into big round biscuits with tea. With a distinctive snarl in his voice, the small man declared, 'There were two of them, I hate them, and I want to snap their little necks. One was tall and dark, the other was about as tall as me, and he had a bit of a paunch.'

Basu was already leaning in with all his attention focused on the words coming out of the man's mouth.

'When did they come here?' Basu asked.

'A few weeks ago. They seemed like nice boys, from nice homes. Little did I know . . .'

'Hmmm.'

'Why the sudden interest in those two?' The pimp was curious.

'They are the flavour of the month.' Sarkar perked up.

'I see, I see . . . may I ask who is funding this great cause?'

'I cannot say.'

'This can't be a one-way street, Basu. You have to meet me halfway.'

'I would . . . I just think you're a sleazy piece of shit pimp.'

As the comment hit home, the man's mouth twisted and

the consternation grew evident on his face. Seeing the effect the words had on him, Basu and Sarkar both broke out in a fit of outrageously loud laughter.

'I'm only kidding Bhai sahib, you're not a sleazy piece of shit at all . . . You're my brother, my partner, my . . .'

'Enough.' The flesh merchant raised his hand stopping them.

'Okay, tell me more,' Basu coaxed.

'Their names were Shakaal and . . . Murli, what was the other fucker's name?'

'I think it was Ajeet, boss.'

'Right! Ajeet and Shakaal. Sons of rabies-infected bitches.'

'I'll get them.' Basu tried to calm him down.

'Bring them to me.'

'What? Out of the question.'

'Listen, those ass-maggots have cost me a lot of business. Too many of my regulars seem to have lost their drive mysteriously after their little escapade. And how will this dhandha run without clients?'

'What about the shame? There is also that, no?' Basu quipped. He was enjoying this. There was more money to be made.

'Arre, that too. The fucking shame. I myself am walking around with a bloody green mug. Look at this . . . look at my neck, the fucking thing is still green. I'm like a bloody fern!'

'Hmmm . . .' Basu said, thoughtfully. Hearing the man swear and whine, Basu had his own personal Fort Knox growing brick by brick in his mind. The man may think he looked like a fern, but to Basu he was a luscious little money plant.

'Stop your hemming and hawing and promise me that you will bring them to me first . . .'

'Listen. It's not that simple . . .'

'Does the other party want you to kill them or capture them?' the pimp interrupted him.

'Kill.'

'There! So all you need to do is catch them for me, bring them here and I will do the killing. See . . . simple.'

'But that raises the question of some kind of compensation for our troubles. After all, you see Sarkar is a growing boy,' Basu said coyly, winking.

'What is money between us? Don't worry. I will pay you. I will pay you well. Just bring them to me.'

Basu triumphantly scratched his privates as he named his price. 'I'll do it for ten.'

'Er, no . . . you'll do it for seven.'

'Nine.'

'Eight . . .'

'Eight and a half . . .'

'Done. Eight and a half for the Anarchists of Mumbai. Bring both those nosey cocksuckers to me. If there are more in their gang bring them too.'

The two famous hit men charged out of the brothel with even greater determination to get the Anarchists.

'These boys are proving to be more profitable than any other racket I've known,' Sarkar said, as they drove off.

'Tell me about it.' Basu grinned, mentally counting the money they were making on the Anarchists.

The grimy underbelly of the city was home to them; they had nestled in its dirty womb since they were boys. They knew every corner, every doorway and every creep behind it. They decided to go about asking them all for more information about their prize prey. Sure enough, wherever they went they were offered more to bring the 'nice young boys' back to that establishment.

Meanwhile, the other investigation was heating up too. Guru was out asking local paan-shop owners if some strange men had come to place a one-time order of paan leaves and raw materials, or perhaps just a huge order of paans. He was pointed to many big shots that had placed large orders for weddings and functions.

'Which bloody street shop makes receipts? This is a wild goose chase. Akram is out of his mind,' thought the disgruntled policeman.

They learnt that the articles for the newspapers to print with cash payments were dropped off and not posted. A call came in the same day, ensuring that the job would be done.

Another tired officer was tasked with tailing Shahnaz, watching her every move and tracking people that she met. Akram felt that she had more to do with the case than she claimed. So the poor chap made trips all over town, from her office to her hairstylist, from her home to her uncle's place, to the various restaurants she would frequent with friends. He also shadowed her while she haggled with vegetable vendors and shopped for groceries.

Shahnaz being Shahnaz realized that she was under surveillance and confronted the fellow outside a restroom in a pub once. He mumbled something about it being for her protection and sped off.

The big man himself was questioning people at the ad agency associated with SHB's ill-fated XS3000 launch. He had a nice long chat with Mr Khanna, the good old boss with the 'Vinci' wall.

Mukherjee on the other hand was busy at the Royal Bharat Chemical Company looking for leads and other dubious-sounding things that policemen are often tasked with searching for. He enjoyed his work despite the dead ends and powered on.

They kept in touch and had a daily meeting to report on their findings. They all went about diligently searching for something, anything, that would give them even an idea about where to look for the famous perpetrators.

Calls came in frequently: ministers, corporate lords, pimps, everybody who was somebody was enquiring about the Anarchists, pushing the cops harder.

Amit Chopra finally went on camera confessing his deeds, how he and the BEIRC chairman were working together. They had been at it for a long time and had many such 'understandings' in different parts of Maharashtra. He begged for forgiveness and a chance to redeem himself.

The police declared a reward for any information leading to the capture of the 'Mumbai Anarchists'.

22. DOUBT

I sat in my chair looking out through the same drawing room window where I had had my epiphany about my purpose in life not long ago. I felt I had come a long way from there.

A few days ago some university students in Kolkata had painted on the glass windows of an imported automobile showroom the word 'Need?'

I wondered what Mr Robin Kapoor, the SHB man, was doing. I thought about what my old boss Mr Khanna would be up to. I thought about Shahnaz and about Dhwani.

I thought about where it would all end, about what we would all become in a few years. Where would we be and what would we be doing? We had enacted some of our Bugs Bunny piano scenes and the banana-plastering exercise was well under way. But was it sustainable?

I called up Shahnaz.

'How are things?' she asked cheerfully.

'I'm okay. I can't decide what to do next.'

'What do you mean?'

'I'm a little lost. How do I tie it all up? Where does it end?'

'Okay, that sounds like fodder for a longer conversation,

one which I unfortunately don't have time for right now. Tell you what, I'll come and see you after my afternoon taping and we'll . . .'

'No, it's all right.' I cut her short.

'I'll speak to you sometime soon.' She sounded apologetic. 'Bye.'

Everything till now had passed in a haze. We had done what we had to when the time was right. Years of anger had taken form. Years of frustration had come to a fruition that few would term ordinary. Unfortunately, in spite of being extraordinary I felt small. I felt like all the actions we had taken were blurring with the passage of time. I stared out of the window looking for some sense of permanence, trying to re-experience the simple joy that we had got from sticking it to the fuckers who had ruined us.

She surprised me when she came by later.

'It'll never die,' she said, quietly.

I looked at her disbelievingly.

'It can't. You're a fool to think that what we have done will die.'

'I know what we've done, but do people understand it?'

'I think they do!'

'Do they know? Do they see what we're all about?'

'I think there's a good number of people out there who have been moved by your thoughts and are beginning to understand what you're saying.'

'We've got quite a name, man! We're celebrities. If people knew who we were, we'd get mobbed every time we stepped out of this place!' Abhay's wisdom sparked forth.

'Here's the thing. I have little money left. I have a lot more that I want to say. Firstly I'm not sure of what to do and secondly . . .'

'I'll chip in, man. Chill.' Abhay offered breezily.

'What?'

'I know a lot of people who would be more than happy to chip in to keep the project afloat,' Shahnaz added.

'How would we ever do that? We're already vigilantes, we're already on the run, how exactly will we canvass for funds?'

'Leave that to me,' she said.

Abhay and I looked at each other disapprovingly.

'It would be the stupidest thing in the world if we got caught trying to raise capital for this.'

'Then what would you like to do? Die without a whimper? Forget the movement?'

The doorbell rang.

'Mr Kumar? Open up. This is the police. We have some questions for you.'

My heart sank. It was quite apparent that we all had the same terrible feeling in the pits of our stomachs.

'Who is it?'

'Advani, from the police. Please, open the door, sir.'

'It isn't over yet. I have a lot more to say. This is just three-fifths of my . . .' I blurted out in a hushed voice to the only two people who probably completely understood how I felt at that time.

'It isn't over. Relax. I'll go in and clear the designs and your papers. Shahnaz, you open the taps in the kitchen to fill the buckets there. I've been meaning to wash them,' said a calm Abhay.

'What's in them? Can't that sort of thing wait?' Shahnaz was confused.

'Sure it can, there are just some remnants of the toxic waste in them.'

'I'll get right to it.' Shahnaz was convinced.

'Are you coming?' the policeman asked again.

I glared at Abhay and then urged them both to run along and attend to the clearing up operations.

'I'll get the door.'

The sound of my own lock coming undone had never been so meaningful to me. I swung it open with my bravest, most innocent face to greet the man of the law. It was similar to my fake smiles and expression of glee from the days I had spent working on things like the infamous Pegasus shorts. It all came back to me now. The façade, the need to lie . . .

'Sir! We thought you were not going to come to the door.'

'How may I help you?' I asked.

'We were just asking people in the building about some untoward activity.'

This doesn't sound so bad. There's doubt in his voice!

'Did you see two men get out of a van in front of your building, a few nights ago, they were in plain clothes . . . but they had buckets and torches with them?'

'No . . . why?'

'Sir, we believe they might have been involved in some criminal activities. You're certain you saw no one?'

'I'm quite sure. But let me ask my flatmate,' I said facetiously as I turned around to yell into the flat.

'Hey Abhay, you heard the gentleman, were there a couple of guys running around with buckets a few nights ago? In front of our building?'

'No, no. You know I go to bed really early,' Abhay said as he emerged from my bedroom.

'Yeah, that's true. Our man Abhay goes to bed really early.'

'Okay. How long have you been living here?'

'Just about a year now.'

'I see. Where do you work?'

'I'm currently looking for a job, my flatmate, that's Abhay, works for a chemical company.'

'Is it the Royal Bharat Chemical Company?' he asked with a glint of hope in his eyes.

'No, not that one.'

'All right, thanks for your help.' Advani was noticeably disappointed.

'We're keeping an eye on this area. There are a few people who claim to have seen some suspicious activities taking place here. If you see or hear anything unusual, please give me a call on my number,' he handed me his card and started to walk over to the next flat. He had a smile on his face, as though he was trying to comfort us.

'What exactly do you suspect is happening around here?' I asked, stopping him in his tracks.

'Something grave, something awful. Just keep a lookout. Your vigilance could help avert disasters, we need responsible citizens like you to help us.'

I shut the door and stepped back into the apartment. I could hardly contain my laughter. Abhay seemed to be smiling through his distress. Despite his watery smile, his tone was accusatory.

'Well, I think it's safe to say that we fucked up somewhere along the way.'

'What could possibly have led them here?' Shahnaz enquired, raising her voice over the noise of the buckets filling with water.

'They have a hotline up and running for informants. It could have been anyone.'

She walked out of the kitchen and sat down with us. 'You have to be more careful.' I saw a deep concern in her eyes as she turned to me and spoke. 'We have to get everything out there. Don't worry about things like money.' She reassured me. She was a source of strength and inspiration.

Abhay just nodded and walked towards the window.

'I told you we should've dumped the buckets,' he said menacingly.

'There was no other option,' I argued.

'We should not have gone to her place, man. We should have just lain low. There are a lot of different ways to do things.'

'Shhh . . . I know this guy,' Shahnaz interrupted.

She had picked up the television remote to raise the volume.

Abhay didn't heed her.

'All I'm saying is that you need to listen to others while planning this. It isn't a one-man show. It's not something only one person can pull off. It's not like you have training or experience in the art of hijacking and mutilating a car!' His eyebrows were raised far beyond I had ever seen them go.

'I realize that . . . we'll plan things better from now on, okay?'

'Thank you!'

'And thank you both for shutting up.' It was Shahnaz's turn to be agitated.

The three of us sat there in the drawing room, looking at the television. They were announcing and presenting 'The Greatest Fashion Show on Earth: Postmodern Style by Wahid Farookh'.

'I know him. He's quite an asshole in real life,' Shahnaz remarked.

'I read his interview in the paper the other day. When is the show?'

'This coming Friday, see they're setting it up at the Oyster Ballroom.'

'Everybody is going to be there. It'll be an extravaganza not to be missed and impossible to forget, when the new WF line makes its way down the ramp behind me.' The adolescent reporter girl could barely contain her excitement.

'To add to the glory of the long anticipated WF creations there will be a host of other attractions to entertain the fortunate swish set that will be here in the Oyster Ballroom of the JW Marriott just a few days from now. Top models are being flown in especially for the show. Earlier today we had a chance to catch up with a few of them, here are the highlights.'

Here come the models.

'I'm standing here with Josh Segal by the pool of the JW Marriott in Mumbai; it is a great feeling to finally meet you Josh!'

'Great to finally meet you too, of course. I only heard of you this morning, from my agent.'

Josh was built like a Greek god who had a gym in his house and lived on steroids. His famous jawline had sold many a watch and pushed many a perfume. He fixed his hair and pulled up his trunks as the giggling reporter girl beside him continued her coy interview.

'Tell us Josh, how does it feel to be in India?'

'It's been a fantastic experience so far. The weather is a little humid, but the girls are very nice.'

'She's gushing, she's going pink for god's sake!' Shahnaz couldn't believe it.

'See this is what we have to compete with to ride the fucking airwaves. I can't watch this shit.' Abhay got up and went to his room.

'There are too many of us who get sucked into this shit. Too many value this.'

Shahnaz looked at me. 'Big wheels are turning?'

I pulled out a cigarette and lit it. Sinking back into my chair I told her to look at the folder that lay on the table in front of her.

'I've decided that I need to get a day job. To keep the war alive, I need to fund it. To fund it, I need a job. I won't go back to work in an ad agency though.'

'How about a bank?' she laughed loudly as I looked back at her in mock anger. It took a while for her to settle down after that; more often than not we were reminded that Shahnaz's favourite comedienne happened to be Shahnaz herself.

'In any case, what does this folder have to do with that?'

'Nothing, my lady. Page three of the folder, quite aptly, contains my answer to Mr Wahid Farookh.'

She flipped to the correct page. She smiled as she read.

'You're a sick, evil man!'

'That's only what my friends say!'

'I love you!' she exclaimed.

'I love you too Shahnaz.' I was chuffed and a wee bit embarrased at my own candour.

I looked at her caress the page and read it over and over again.

'This will be magnificent, if you pull it off properly . . .'

'We will. Hey Abhay . . .'

He looked away from the television.

'What's with all the racket?'

'Nothing, man. Just get your suit ready. We have a party to gatecrash.'

At first he didn't quite understand. His familiar look of bewilderment changed to a knowing smile when he saw Shahnaz and me waiting for him to catch on. She tossed the folder up to him.

He pulled it open with excitement and read out the heading: 'A model solution.'

23. A MODEL SOLUTION

My Caulfieldesque questioning of what was defined as joy had often been the cause for annoyance and anguish to those who happened to associate with me. I had ruined countless get-togethers and birthday parties with my unwillingness to accept happiness passed around in 'stylish' martini glasses.

I had mocked the giggling cousins for their expression of glee upon receiving Gucci shoes and Prada bags. I had even been forced to play the game. I had bought gifts for those who mattered to me, keeping in mind that they would value a certain brand. It used to eat me up, this pandering to what was considered 'fashionable' and cool.

The answer was clear. In a society where certain standards for looks, appearances and even accents for talking are so markedly defined in categories of acceptable and deplorable, it is difficult for children to grow up without wanting certain things or wanting to be a particular way. Seeking John Ab's abs, Katrina's butt, Zayed Khan's jacket ... shopping at Tommy-Go-Figure and Scabtree and Evelyn.

Why should anyone tell you what to wear? Who to look like or what to be?

It saddened me to see people waste their lives away. If I asked them what they had achieved, their response would be a list of brand names or designers, in alphabetical order. There are no fat models in this town.

Self-improvement magazines and books sell out the moment they hit the stands.

There's nothing wrong with improving yourself. However, the parameters that you work on and the aspects that you attempt to improve ought to be your own. After all, it is your body. It is your choice to change and modify. The standards and the source of the standards by which we end up judging ourselves need questioning and analysis. Why the fuck should it be 36–24–36?

So the giggling cousins pack the sweaty gyms while friends of fashion hit the salons. People are discriminated against on the basis of the shoes they buy and the pens they use. There are haves and have-nots. Everyone has their own complex. Everyone is screaming inside.

And for what? The scam of an era, concocted by the scum of the earth, strings and beads put together for people to walk about in, in the name of high fashion.

Not on our watch. No.

Thanks to Shahnaz we were able to get in a few days early, to check out the preparations for the show and decide our course of action. And then, in accordance with our very detailed plans we all reported at battle stations on the night of the event. We were on the esteemed guest list as representatives of a famous blog run by 'LA-based plastic surgeons'. I was a 'contributing editor' on ScalpelGorgeous.com. Our IDs were works of art. Shahnaz, of course, went as Shahnaz. It was a magnificent ballroom and the security was really tight. A lot of Page Three regulars were expected to land up and support Farookh. Unlike the other occasions, this time we would have to be in the ballroom through the evening. Which meant we would have to blend in.

Wahid Farookh was in his element. He sprung about the room like a praying mantis. Wahid worked the crowd, spending the obligatory two minutes with each group. He was brimming with confidence and oozing charm. We stood by the bar watching the madness as it grew into an uncontrollable frenzy of laughter and merriment. Inane tales and anecdotes that began and ended nowhere were celebrated out of compulsion and ignorance. One couldn't help but overhear some of the gems from the evening.

'So I told the waiter that this is not a Merlot,' one diamond-encrusted lady crowed, 'and he turns to me with the most unbelievable audacity and says, "Merlot hai, ma'am, Pinot Merlot".' With her eyes widening to make the point, she concluded, 'The daft fellow got confused between a Pinot and a Merlot, can you believe that?' Her friends burst out into gales of laughter at the waiter's ignorance.

'And then I told Veer to just sell the goddam horse, so he did! Now his daughter doesn't have a horse but she's still sleeping with that jockey!' said one ex-maharaja chuckling at his friend's misfortune.

High society got higher as the corks flew about. Until someone finally remembered why they had all gathered at the hotel that night.

'Ladies and gentlemen, if you could please settle down at your tables, we'll begin the show in a few moments,' the microphone controller snuck in rather merrily.

What the horse-trading Pinot-pushers didn't know is that during their pre-party party, Abhay had paid the dressing rooms a visit. He had made his way through security as one of their own. His penchant for military movies surfaced yet again as he chose to be Agent Rathore of RAW, inspecting the premises for explosives and other potentially harmful devices. The beautiful people stepped aside for his search, during which he went on to make a few adjustments to the clothing for the evening. He was armed with a pair of scissors for accentuating snips and a dash of itching powder, for flavour.

I went back up near the control room, ready with my part of the ruse.

The show started with some catchy music filling up the room. It comprised the generic house-trance sounds that were difficult to tell apart. The beat kicked in prominently and one by one, the models made their way on to the ramp.

They cat-walked and mock-snarled, enticing the crowd. They took their sex appeal and amplified it by subtly toying with their tongues and fixing their dresses. Some of them scratched themselves as they walked by. The scratching and constant adjustment, along with Abhay's creative contributions to the lingerie, led to an embarrassing situation for three models who had walked out together. Their excuses for bras fell to the floor. One was flung sideways out into the audience. The crowd laughed and whistles matched every beat of the soundtrack. Wahid Farookh was on his feet, livid. His voice rose with every slipping bra, with every scratching model.

'What the fuck is going on?'

'What does she think she's doing throwing that top off! She'll never work with anyone I know ever again.'

'Why are all their dresses coming apart?'

And finally, 'Stop the fucking show!'

The flashbulb police had a field day with the sights and sounds at the famous venue.

The models started itching and scratching on stage, at first mildly, but then building up into a violent outbreak. Some embarrassed models ran back to the dressing rooms in tears. Others who tried to brave the itching were visibly uncomfortable.

'What the hell is going on? What's wrong with my models?'

Wahid Farookh whipped out his phone and started yelling at someone. 'What is going on back there? Why are the clothes falling off? Don't tell me you don't know because I will fire you immediately . . . This is my life's work here you fool! What the fuck is wrong with you people?'

The scratching made the dresses move and they continued to come loose because of Abhay's fashionable improvisations. The snips grew larger as the models scratched. Flashes went off insanely as shocked owners held on to skirts that started to fall apart and straps that gave way as they ran back, out of sight.

The lights went out.

A projection rose up behind the ramp. This is what it said in bold:

Slide 1:
'WE REJECT YOUR DESIGNS'

Slide 2:
'NO ONE TELLS ME WHAT TO LOOK LIKE'

Slide 3:
'WELCOME TO THE REAL POSTMODERN STYLE, FAKERS'

Slide 4:
'YOUR ANARCHISTS LOVE YOU, DAHLING!'

They lined us all up for preliminary questioning. I was smooth. Our site had been set up well before. Googling us would yield a selection of eclectic articles compiled from Wikipedia and our own research. The only thing missing was a Facebook group dedicated to us.

We walked out triumphantly after completing our assault on the fuming fashion world. I could have sworn I heard a *Reservoir Dogs* theme kick in, Abhay had his Michael Madsen look on his face as we started to cross the road, a car drove by really fast in front of us and splashed muddy water all over our suits. The *Reservoir Dogs* theme and looks came to a cruel halt, as the car sped away.

We were in the dirt now. We were cleaning it up.

24. SOME REUNIONS ARE BEST AVOIDED

After the fashion show incident, we had to cut back on activities for a while as the security in and around our neighbourhood had increased to near siege levels. There were policemen on patrol till late in the night.

However, the news reports did not die. Dhwani Sinha had regular stories covering our actions. Shahnaz, too, played dedications to the Anarchists on her show quite regularly.

So it was quite an achievement that we were able to pull off the paint-bomb attack. For weeks Abhay and I had taken turns to travel the line and time the journey so that we could time the paint attack just right. Assembling everything without drawing attention had been excruciating. But we had done it in the end.

I stood at the platform watching the chaos mount, congratulating myself.

All the attention and efforts of the police and medics were focused in a central area.

'It's only paint,' the medics reassured the weeping men and women.

They had a guy appointed to just run around telling everyone that they were going to be fine. I walked away slowly, to make my way out of the station, smoking my cigarette. I called Abhay on his cell to let him know that he could pick me up from the western exit.

'I'll be near the movie theatre entrance in about five minutes. Can you make it there by then?'

'I can. But I won't,' he said.

'What?' I kept walking, looking over my shoulder every now and then.

'I won't,' he said sternly.

'Why? Is someone following you? Is everything all right?'

'Oh, it's all good.'

'Well then what is it?'

'We're Anarchists, Pranav. We listen to no one.'

'Right, see you there in a bit, jackass.'

'See you.' He chuckled as we cut the phone.

The media had also arrived at the site. Interviews had begun and the usual confusion was being recorded in high definition. I smiled to myself and turned to exit the station, when I heard a very familiar voice from behind me. It had stayed with me ever since the first time I had heard it.

'You aren't going to colour me eh, Anarchist?'

It was the murderer in the Fiat who had threatened me once. I turned around and looked him in the eye. My heart was on a treadmill to hell.

'Excuse me? I'm sorry you've got the wrong guy . . .'

Before I finished that sentence, I felt a hard knock on my head. A flash of blinding pain and I fell to my knees with the force of the blow. Touching the spot where I had been hit I realized it was moist. Then it happened again.

Everything faded into black.

25. THE SILO

I woke up coughing, choking. There were fumes of some kind rising up around me. I could smell sewage, as if it were climbing slowly into my lungs. My arms were tied behind my back. I lay on the floor, my back to the wall. I could taste blood in my mouth. I looked around the room and in the corner there lay another man. He too was bound like me.

I could barely speak. The room was blurry to my eyes. I struggled to gain my senses.

Only one thought was clear. They had caught us. They had tracked us down.

Either that or this was a terrible nightmare. I sat up in the dank room. The smell grew worse as I looked around for signs of my captors. The man beside me didn't even stir as I moaned in pain.

'Are you okay?' I groaned out to him, thankful that I had someone else here with me.

There was no answer. He was still unconscious.

I looked around at the room we were in. The walls were discoloured. There was a spattering of red on some sections.

There were cracks all over the place. The floor was filthy. Was it oil that lay in front of me? I dared not touch it or go closer.

I remembered the men at the railway station. I remembered the knock on my head. Suddenly, I was aware of it again. Suddenly, it hurt all over again.

'I said are you okay?' I cried in desperation.

Even though I couldn't see the man's face, I knew it was not Abhay. But the fear persisted . . . Did they get him too? What about Shahnaz?

Wherever they are, I hope they are luckier than me, I thought.

I tried standing up but didn't succeed. My legs ached and shivered uncontrollably when I tried to pull myself up. I gave up and fell back on the floor, taking deep breaths.

My heart stopped when I heard the door open. Three distinct bars of metal and then it creaked forward. The theatrical opening was punctuated by scraping footsteps on a grimy floor. I looked up and saw his feet first; I panned up slowly, straining my neck.

'I'm not just a tie-shirt,' he shouted.

'I'm not just a tie-shirt,' he laughed.

I could see his face now. Spit flew out from between his dirty teeth as he said those words repeatedly.

'Remember? That's all you said, as we carried your fat ass out of the station.'

'How's the head now that we've used it like a cricket ball?' his half-witted sidekick quipped as he strolled in behind Basu.

'How is the Anarchist's concussion?' they taunted me.

Ignoring them I tried getting up again, only to discover more parts of my body that were in pain, broken I was convinced. What had this sadistic human garbage done to me?

The man bent over me and sneered. 'I don't like your face when it's like this . . . Are you scowling at me?'

'Why have you brought me here?' I asked as I struggled against the bonds on my wrists.

'Why does anyone do anything?'

'You haven't even got the right guy. I'm not an anarchist. Whoever is paying you will be disappointed.' I could barely whisper. Each breath of mine hurt my throat.

The playful captors continued. How happy they were to see me up. How pleased they were to see me trying to escape my bonds, to call for help.

'I'm sure that at least one of you is an Anarchist.'

He stepped back and pulled out a gun from his pants, displaying his cowboy-like prowess by flipping it around in circles around his fat pointing finger. He then proceeded to straighten his moustache with the tip of the weapon. The other guy just watched with a perverse curiosity. He looked like he was in awe of what his boss was doing. I pitied them both. I pitied the crumbling wall. He fired two shots into it.

'Are you even listening to us, son? Tell us who you really are or . . .'

The squeaky guy spoke from behind him.

'This is interesting, boss. I wonder if our social worker man here ever thought he would be caught.' He walked up to me and peered into my eyes.

'He's too arrogant. Even now, all tied up and bleeding but look at that scowl. I'll tell you the problem. He's been loved too much by his mother. I bet she told you that you were special, right?'

'I'm sure she did. She must have told him that everyone wants to hear from him, as she fed him gajar ka halwa with little crushed almonds on top of it.' Basu picked up where Sarkar left off.

'Fucking moron. Your mother was wrong. Why did you poke your nose in Mr Chopra's business?'

'I don't know who or what you're talking about. Let me go, I am not who you're looking for.'

'We'll just see about that.' He was getting aggravated.

I could see he was enjoying my anguish. The grin on his face widened. The other guy stepped forward and kicked me in my stomach. I couldn't recognize the animal howl that broke free from my throat as my body felt like it had burst into flames below my chest.

'Tell us who you are. Are you not the fucking Anarchist running around, throwing shit at fuckers, painting their sad faces green? Tell us or this guy is going to feel a nice sting inside his pink and fluffy guts.'

I looked at my cellmate. I stared at the spattering on the walls. The doorway behind them was a few feet away. It seemed like a mile. What would I not give to see what was outside?

I looked back at his ugly mug and said nothing.

He kicked me again. The black leather shoes dug in deep. I could feel bile in my gullet, bubbling up slowly; a terrible taste filled my mouth.

He clicked his gun and stepped back.

'We've spent too much time trying to wake you fuckers up.'

'What kind of tough guys, what kind of big-time perpetrators can't take a hit on the head?' they teased.

'I'm tired of waiting. I need an answer for my people quickly. In any case they are on their way, they'll recognize you for sure. It would be best if you tell me who you are instead of prolonging your misery.'

I spat to my left. There wasn't enough strength in me to throw what I had to far enough. It fell on my shoulder and I looked at it, disgusted.

Basu's angry rant gave way to a calm, teacher-like manner. He walked up and knelt in front of me.

'I am going to shoot this man now. Unless you tell me who you are and confess to being the Anarchists. Both of you.'

He got up and moved up to the guy next to me.

They picked him up and dragged him closer to me. He was limp and seemed to be out cold. I just stared back at them blankly. If only they hadn't been enjoying themselves so much.

'I hate to say this, but I'm going to count to seven. If I don't hear from you by then, I will shoot him, first in the stomach, then in his feet and finally in the head.'

'Why seven boss?'

'Shut the fuck up, we don't have time for ten.'

'You don't scare me,' I said.

'One!'

'Two!'

The rubber had met the road for a second time. Things had taken a turn for the worse.

I am here because of my actions alone, I thought to myself. This is not going to happen. I can't let this happen.

'Three!'

'Four!'

'Shoot him now, boss, this chap doesn't seem to care.'

'Let him go,' I cried.

'Five! Two more and this place will soon smell a lot worse!'

Tears trickled down my face. I have to do the right thing; I can't let this man die.

'Stop it. Stop. He's not an Anarchist. I am.'

Their faces lit up as I said those words.

'Say that again! Say that again!'

'I am the Anarchist, you piece of shit. I am. Not this man.'

He looked like a bowler after taking a hat-trick. Pumping his fists and clapping loudly.

'It worked!'

I looked at him as he said this.

'I fucked you over! I fucked you over!'

What the hell were these two idiots talking about?

What happened next will remain with me as one of the worst moments in my life, for time immemorial. Forever.

He stopped laughing and rejoicing and in a matter of two seconds, emptied as many bullets from his pistol into the man lying not more than a few inches away from me.

I closed my eyes and prayed that what was happening was just my imagination. That it was some kind of cruel joke.

It was not.

'That's twice boss. You've killed this fucker twice now!'

They had tricked me. The other man in the room had been dead long before they had caught and tortured me.

'We've got it on tape! We've got you saying it on tape! You're the Anarchist!'

I pulled myself up to the other man and tugged on his arm. It was as limp as before.

I had never been around guns. In fact the only time someone had threatened me, it had been the same creeps. Now they had me at their mercy again. There were no policemen down the road. There was no one around.

'I'm going to make a lot of money off you, son.'

'The right people will pay through their noses for a shot at you.'

'They all got what they deserved,' I said.

'Yes, they did . . . and now it's your turn.'

With that he got up, scratching his belly. The smug look of contentment on his face turned to a genuine smile as he pulled out his gun again and walked towards me.

I didn't flinch. If this is what you get for trying to change things, then so be it. If this is my destiny, to be killed by this murderer, then so be it. I have done what I wanted to. I have done most of what I wanted to. Wait. There's a lot more that I want to do. There's a lot more. He kicked the dirty puddle of liquid that lay in front of me. It flew up and made its mark on my face and shirt as I closed my eyes.

I didn't show him any weakness. I didn't beg for mercy. I didn't ask for 'forgiveness'. He put the gun on my right temple and whispered in my left ear. I will never forget that whiff of rotting teeth and rancid food from his breath. I will never forget those words.

'You should have stayed in your tower, with your silk tie

and your expensive pen. I am the one who makes the changes around here. No one but I, no one can do anything in this town, but me.'

I looked back at him angrily, our eyes piercing each other's.

'It's mine. It's all mine,' he continued calmly. 'You're going to pay when the chemical seth's people and my friends from good old Mariana get here.'

He hit me hard on my head with the butt of his gun and walked away.

He shot at the poor dead man next to me, again.

'That's three times!' he exclaimed.

I heard the triple lock come back on.

Would I die with honour? Was this honour?

The wait inside the room gave me some time to think. It gave me time to assess the things I had done. The earlier part of my life juxtaposed against what it was now painted an interesting picture. Some would say I was a failure who lost his way. Others might applaud me for my direction. I wished that the latter would be a more common sentiment.

For myself, I had no complaints. I could not have gone with the flow. I didn't.

There had been a huge circus around each of our activities. Each of our protests had been viewed, dissected and played up adequately. Were they really worthy? Was there real merit in what we had done or was it just the fodder that a country with multiple twenty-four-hour news channels needed to survive?

I'd like to believe there was more that we achieved. I know we were more than fillers. I know we had reached out to a lot of people, largely the younger generation, people who saw what they were being fed, and by whom.

From all my readings and understanding of anarchist movements, one thing was clear: a lot of them didn't succeed because there was not much to tie their actions together and present them as a clear ideology, for the appreciation and understanding of someone who was not a part of the movement, yet. A lot of them had been violent. A lot of them had killed for causes. Many had leaders, like the original granddaddy of all anarchists—Bakunin. Bakunin was a man with strong beliefs and immense passion for them. He was not a great writer or conveyor of ideas though. From what I had read of his work, he seemed to be writing against a system passionately. Tearing down certain pillars of thought. He didn't sum it all up for me. He didn't tell me what he wanted in the long run. He wanted change and improvement. He didn't tell me what exactly that would entail.

Marx on the other hand was his rival and opposite. He was hungry for power and had a grip on all the factors that would get him that. He seemed to be a visionary with a clear plan.

The results of their actions and the total that their lives had led to indicated that one approach was perhaps better. Not the ideology or concept itself, but the presentation and accumulation of ideas. They were both revolutionaries. Was I a revolutionary? I couldn't dream of comparing myself to Marx and Bakunin. I had only just begun my assault on a generation of decadence. There was a long way to go and much to learn and understand. There were many roads left to walk. It all had to start again.

I got up from my paan-spit-drenched corner. My blood mixed with the orange remains of someone's leafy discharge. I tried freeing my arms. The coarse ropes dug into my skin. This had to be done.

I fought through and managed to get some leeway. There was hope under my skin. I moved more violently now. I could hear voices outside. They were probably laughing about how they had fooled me into my 'confession' by threatening to kill a dead man. I wanted to put an end to their incessant, insipid drivel. I wanted to get outside and pick up that gun he had hit me with and make him swallow it in pieces.

They had been careless. The knots were loose. I just hadn't noticed it before. I freed my hands.

Never before had I been so aware of my limbs. I rubbed the life back into my hands that burned as the blood flowed into them. I tentatively tried taking a few steps, testing my legs. A few minutes of stumbling around and I could feel my stability returning. I was still dizzy but grateful for the ability to walk. I stood on the side that the door opened. The trick had worked in numerous movies, perhaps it would work for me too. I stood pressed up against the wall, waiting for one of the two goons to walk in. The wait was agonizing.

I pictured myself lunging towards him, knocking him to the ground and then choking the life out of him with the ropes he had bound me with.

'See yourself winning. See yourself scoring a goal and then do it,' my eighth-grade football coach's voice rang in my head. For some reason this felt like a game of football to me. Tackle the forward, get the ball and go shoot the other guy.

I heard the whistle blow. It had three clangs that I no longer feared.

The door swung forward and he said: 'They're on their way, princess.'

Before he realized that I had freed myself, I leapt on him from behind and pushed his balding head into the wall. He was shaken by the collision and held his head. I took the opportunity and learnt that my greatest weapon in this scenario would be the wall itself. I held him by his collar and banged him into the wall again. This was Sarkar, of 'Basu and Sarkar' fame. There was no sign of the boss. He tried calling out to him. My rage knew no bounds and my fists would not stop as I tried each and every way to hurt him. I kicked him in his stomach as he had done to me. I punched him in his face only to step back in agony myself. I kicked him in the face. He was now buckling under the beating, he was writhing in pain. I saw him reach for his pants, to pull out his gun. I hit him in the back and pulled out the gun myself. I never thought I was capable of such an assault. I wiped my mouth and looked down at the whimpering bastard before me.

'Where's your fucking cellphone?'

I reached into his pocket and pulled out his cellphone. He tried lifting himself up. I decided the only way to ensure that he would not move would be to stand on his back. That calmed him down a bit. He seemed to be at rest now.

'I'll show you motherfuckers what I can do.' I was a different person.

I jumped on his back and tripped as I came down. The impact would still have hurt. The style of the battering didn't matter; all I wanted was to put this man in a world of pain, and then some.

His cries were getting louder. I pulled off his shoes and removed his filthy socks. One of them was not enough to stuff his enormous mouth. I put both of them in and tied his mouth with the rope they had tied me with. I then tied his hands behind him and left him the way they had kept me after kicking him in his face another time. I locked the door behind me.

I found myself in a dark corridor. It looked like the inside of an abandoned grain silo. We must be far out of town I thought. I started walking towards the light.

I now had Sarkar's gun and his cellphone. I put the phone on silent and made for the door.

I would never let anyone forget about the Amit Chopra incident. I would never let anyone forget about the SHB event. I would punish the pimps and their patrons some more. I would do more. I reached the large door and peered out through the tiny opening. He was walking right towards me up the small hill we were on. It was dry outside and I could see him through the swirls of rising dust. He was coming back to the silo.

I stepped back, checked the gun and pointed it towards the doorway, expecting him to walk through: my unsuspecting and hopefully hapless target. I heard a thump on the outside of the door and I saw his hirsute hand push it open. I took a deep breath and aimed my gun at him. He didn't see me.

He walked in and stopped. I think he sensed that something was amiss. Maybe the light from the outside had lit up my cold steely weapon. There was no time to wait. No time for an old Western-style shootout. I had the upper hand. I was the victim. I took the shot. Right in his thigh, then in his miserable shins. He shouted in pain as he fell to the ground, reaching for his gun. I ran forward and kicked him hard on his chin. He fell back and cried in agony. I kicked him in his wounded thigh.

Thank you Coach Chakravarty.

'You can't kill me! You can't kill me!' he shrieked.

'Who wants to?' I smiled.

I pulled him up and punched him repeatedly in his face, with all my might. It was like a mace after a while, my arm was numb and my fist was covered in blood. Was it all mine? No, of course not.

I took out his gun and kept it aside. I was not done with the rat.

'Whose town is this, motherfucker?' I yelled.

There was no answer. He could not speak. He just gnashed his teeth and tried to stop his eyes from rolling. I punched him again with all my strength. He fell back on the ground with a loud thud. On the floor he swayed from side to side, he clutched his leg.

He called out to Sarkar, abusing him.

'He's going to be a while.' I took his phone away too.

He looked up at me, defeated, crying in pain.

'Looks like a tie-shirt fucked you over.'

I pulled out Sarkar's cellphone and put in a call to Abhay. I wondered where he was and if he was all right.

He answered the phone.

'Brother,' I said.

'Pranav! Where the fuck are you? We've been looking all over for you.'

I assumed he meant Shahnaz and himself. Later, I would find out that my cautious Tamilian housemate had done more that just that.

'I'm fine, I'm fine now. I was . . . it's a long story. Come and get me.'

Pushing the door wide open, I stepped out from the silo. The bright sun warmed my face as I winced in the intensity of the glorious light.

'Where are you?'

'I'm at a grain silo near Chinchpokhli, I think. You'll have to come and get me. I'm in no condition to make it out of here myself.'

'We'll be there in no time. Hang tight, man.'

'They will come for you too. You're going to pay.' I turned and told Basu, who was now trying to drag himself towards me. Watching them inch dangerously close to me, I kicked his dirty hands away.

I sat outside on a boulder. Looking out towards the gate. Waiting for my friends to come for me.

I turned back every now and then, to keep an eye on the snake, coiling up behind me. I thought I'd have to be inhuman to be enjoying the sweet sounds of his distress.

I got up and walked back towards him. I looked down at him and asked him how he had found me. How did he know I was one of the Anarchists?

'Tell me,' I pressed on his hand with my foot, slowly increasing the weight, as he shouted.

'We got a tip. We got a tip from the police.'

'What? Don't fucking lie . . .'

'No. It's the truth. Our guy told us that they suspected a particular locality, that they were watching people over there closely.'

'And . . .?'

'My partner and I were just following people randomly . . . we happened to follow you two days ago. You never leave the building that early . . . we just followed you and found out who you were.'

'Coincidence?'

'Yes, unlucky coincidence.'

'Fuckers . . .' I pulled my foot off.

I could hear sirens in the distance.

What was going on?

I could now see a string of white Sumos racing towards the gates.

They screeched as they turned in, I waved out to them. This was it. One form of the game was over.

'Even they know who you are now . . . even they know who you are!' Basu laughed. 'You're going where I'm going,' he said.

'We'll see about that.' I sat down on the boulder and waited for them to drive up beside me.

They all stepped out together. Shahnaz, Abhay and Inspector Akram.

My friends came and hugged me. I could only tell them repeatedly that I was fine. They didn't believe me.

'What the hell happened?'

'They caught me. They brought me here. It's all a long, sick story.'

'Well you're a fucking hero.'

'I'm not . . .'

I looked at Inspector Akram as he walked towards me.

'You guys are a real pain in the ass,' he said. 'Are you all right, Pranav?'

'I'm fine, sir, I'm fine.'

The troops ran into the silo, arresting a lame Basu and a gagged Sarkar.

'I told them everything. We're in trouble too.' Abhay mentioned sheepishly.

'I don't care.' I smiled as I sat reunited with my friends, watching the two goons being carried away by the authorities.

'We'll fix it,' I said. 'That's what we do.'

I asked Akram and his men to wait around at the storage unit, for the people who had paid for our capture. I believe they were caught and brought to book too. We were whisked away well before.

26. MY FAVOURITE CELL

At least it wasn't the first time I was in a cell. At least the smell was bearable. There were no corpses cramping my style. I sat alone on the rickety bench.

We had made the true big time in the past few months. We were all over the news. We were the Anarchists who had emerged victorious, capturing two of the Mumbai Police's most wanted criminals.

Our actions had brought us punishments too. Those who were baying for our blood, all the egos we had trampled, sought their revenge. We were to be in the 'protection and confines' of the Mumbai Police for two years each. Destruction of public and private property was all they could throw at us. It was true, our radical actions had had some far-reaching consequences and we had upset enough people to have us locked up for some time. The companies sent their lawyers for our money. We got representation too.

I sat in my jail cell, reading the newspaper. There were reports of protests from all over the country in support of Pranav, Shahnaz and Abhay, the Anarchists of Mumbai.

I wondered if those two were reading the papers and enjoying their stay as much as I was.

The megalomaniac in me was appeased. The Anarchist felt a little satisfied. I constantly wondered how I could keep the ideas alive and push them more, even while I was in prison. We received hundreds of letters every day, most of them commending our actions, others aimed to continue the debate that we had started. We tried our best to answer them all. Some kids set up a website and came to us looking for blog-like posts. We gave them those too. Dhwani Sinha did a feature on us, with in-depth interviews with the 'rebel TV executive' Shahnaz and Abhay the 'chemical engineer whose ingenious concoction had left many green in the face'.

The days went by and I started writing regularly again. I had befriended a few policemen. Mukherjee, Guru and Advani were great chaps. Akram too was a stern but solid man. He made sure we were looked after. I got a little desk moved in to aid me with my writing. It was removed after a month, when a senior minister objected to the 'preferential treatment' that we were receiving. It did not matter much. I continued with my pen and loose papers on the hard floor. The place was not very clean and the food was ridiculously bad. I tried my best to make the most of the time I had to serve. I dropped pounds like no one's business, but I gained weight. This was the new heavy. I was the new heavy. My gait changed. I heard music when I walked again. Where the hell was I going? I had seven steps to pace up and down in my tiny cell. It was a victorious walk though. It was regal. Punk regal.

They caught the policeman who had 'shared' information with Basu and Sarkar. They were all given juicy sentences. Amit Chopra and the distinguished gentlemen from Mariana too had gotten themselves into a lot more trouble.

My parents visited every week. My mother didn't really understand why I had done some of the things for which I was in jail. She wanted me to be at peace with myself and the world. I just told her that her 'live and let live' philosophy was more dangerous than mine. She differed again, but supported me all the same. There was no gajar ka halwa, but the cakes were amazing. And they weren't seasonal. They were reluctantly proud of their famous son, my loving parents.

I even received a note from my old office out of the clear blue sky. It was not signed personally but I guessed who it was from. It was on the company letterhead with just these three words.

'Keep selling, Pranav.'

One fateful Thursday I was told I had an important visitor. A respected book editor from a publishing house that I had been to before I began my life as an Anarchist wanted to meet with me. He brought with him a copy of the essays that I had shared with him.

Mr Malhotra seemed to be happy to see me.

'It's great to meet you again.'

'Likewise,' I said in my most businesslike tone.

'My name is Malhotra . . .'

He seemed a bit uncomfortable and scrambled to adjust the papers in his hands as they started slipping out.

'How can I help you? I was told you have been trying to see me for a while now.'

'Yes, yes, Mr Kumar.'

'Tell me.'

'The thing is, well actually you see . . . the thing is we'd like you to write a book for us.'

'You want me to write a book?' I tried acting surprised.

'Yes, we'd like you to write for us.'

I played along with glee.

'And what would this book be about?'

'Oh, it could be a collection of your essays. Your thoughts on what we have become and what we could be . . . as a society . . .'

'That sounds more like social commentary, not really a story. Is there really a market for that?'

He smiled as he recognized our earlier conversation.

'I know how I sounded then. I am sorry about that. I'm ashamed to be asking you now, given how dismissive I was when I first met you.'

'I see. But I'm no historian or sociologist . . . where's my credibility?'

Malhotra smiled as he leaned forward.

'You know you aren't the same person who came to me with the folder of essays. You were no one then. You hadn't done anything, no one knew you, your thoughts weren't of interest to anyone. But that is not the case today. You are somebody now. People want to hear what you have to say. You were brave enough to take on the system. That's your credibility. That's why I am here. To take your thoughts to the people who want to hear from you, who want to know you better. We want you to write about your experiences, we want you to share what it was like to do the things that you did. You have a voice now, you earned it. You are the Anarchist, and this is your chance to make people understand your message.'

I looked up at him, dropping the disinterested act.

'You're right. You're damn right.'

This was going to be a good ride after all.